"I'm just convinced that the closer we become, the more danger you'll be in."

"What do you mean by danger? You think the kidnapper will threaten us again? Surely he's off somewhere spending the ransom money, not plotting more evil."

"That would be the logical assumption," Rafe agreed. "I know in my head that the threat to you is over...yet I can't help feeling that..."

"That what?" Rhianna prodded. "That I'm still in danger?"

"I'd feel better if you stayed close by."

She smiled at him. "I'm living in your house, lying in your bed. How much closer do you want me?"

"Let me show you." He tugged the towel loose from between her breasts and she rolled into his arms....

Dear Harlequin Intrigue Reader,

The holidays are upon us again. This year, remember to give yourself a gift—the gift of great romantic suspense from Harlequin Intrigue!

In the exciting conclusion to TEXAS CONFIDENTIAL, *The Outsider's Redemption* (#593) by Joanna Wayne, Cody Gannon must make a life-and-death decision. Should he trust his fellow agents even though there may be a traitor among their ranks? Or should he trust Sarah Rand, a pregnant single mother-to-be, who may be as deadly as she is beautiful?

Another of THE SUTTON BABIES is on the way, in *Lullaby and Goodnight* (#594) by Susan Kearney. When Rafe Sutton learns Rhianna McCloud is about to have his baby, his honor demands that he protect her from a determined and mysterious stalker. But Rafe must also discover the stalker's connection to the Sutton family—before it's too late!

An unlikely partnership is forged in *To Die For* (#595) by Sharon Green. Tanda Grail is determined to find her brother's killer. Detective Mike Gerard doesn't want a woman distracting him while on a case. But when push comes to shove, is it Mike's desire to catch a killer that propels him, or his desire for Tanda?

First-time Harlequin Intrigue author Morgan Hayes makes her debut with *Tall, Dark and Wanted* (#596). Policewoman Molly Sparling refuses to believe Mitch Drake is dead. Her former flame and love of her life is missing from Witness Protection, but her superior tracking skills find him hiding out. While the cop in her wants to bring him in, the woman in her wants him to trust her. But Mitch just plain wants her back....

Wishing you the happiest of holidays from all of us at Harlequin Intrigue!

Sincerely,

Denise O'Sullivan
Associate Senior Editor
Harlequin Intrigue

LULLABY AND GOODNIGHT
SUSAN KEARNEY

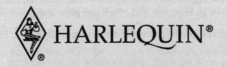

HARLEQUIN®

TORONTO • NEW YORK • LONDON
AMSTERDAM • PARIS • SYDNEY • HAMBURG
STOCKHOLM • ATHENS • TOKYO • MILAN • MADRID
PRAGUE • WARSAW • BUDAPEST • AUCKLAND

ISBN 0-373-22594-6

LULLABY AND GOODNIGHT

Copyright © 2000 by Susan Hope Kearney

Visit us at www.eHarlequin.com

Printed in U.S.A.

ABOUT THE AUTHOR

Susan Kearney used to set herself on fire four times a day; now she does something really hot—she writes romantic suspense. While she no longer performs her signature fire dive, she never runs out of ideas for characters and plots. A business graduate from the University of Michigan, Susan now writes full-time. She resides in a small town outside Tampa, Florida, with her husband and children, and a spoiled Boston terrier. She's currently plotting her way through her next novel.

Books by Susan Kearney

HARLEQUIN INTRIGUE

*The Sutton Babies

Don't miss any of our special offers. Write to us at the following address for information on our newest releases.

Harlequin Reader Service
U.S.: 3010 Walden Ave., P.O. Box 1325, Buffalo, NY 14269
Canadian: P.O. Box 609, Fort Erie, Ont. L2A 5X3

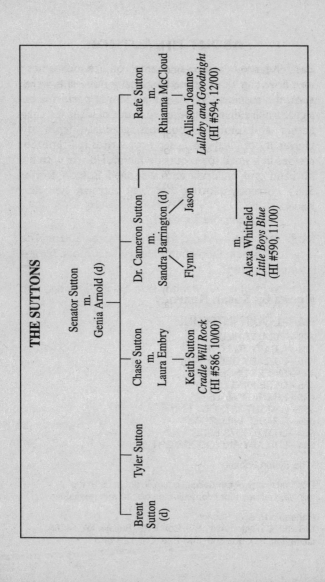

THE SUTTONS

Senator Sutton
m.
Genia Arnold (d)

Brent Sutton (d)

Tyler Sutton

Chase Sutton
m.
Laura Embry

Keith Sutton
Cradle Will Rock
(HI #586, 10/00)

Dr. Cameron Sutton
m.
Sandra Barrington (d)

Flynn

Jason

m.
Alexa Whitfield
Little Boys Blue
(HI #590, 11/00)

Rafe Sutton
m.
Rhianna McCloud

Allison Joanne
Lullaby and Goodnight
(HI #594, 12/00)

CAST OF CHARACTERS

Rafe Sutton—Determined to remain a bachelor, torn between his past and his present, he will have to make the most difficult decision of his life.

Rhianna McCloud—Gutsy, independent and running scared, she turns to Rafe for help. But will Rafe's involvement cause her to lose her precious baby?

Hal Stone—A wealthy neighbor who suspiciously profits from the Suttons' losses.

Janet Stone—Hal's wife. A bimbo blonde? Or is she much more than she appears?

Judge Stewart—An old friend of Senator Sutton. The judge offers help just when Rafe needs it most. Yet are his motives pure?

Duncan Phillip—A wealthy horse breeder who wants to marry Rhianna. Has he his own reasons for wishing Rhianna harm?

For Marty and Steve.

Prologue

In Rhianna McCloud's hands rested the fate of her unborn child. The power to save and protect. Or the power to make a deadly mistake.

She vowed not to panic as she once again checked her truck's rearview mirror. Rhianna swung in a left-hand turn toward Denver, hoping city streets and eye-witnesses might deter her pursuer. She prayed her leaky radiator would hold out, that her rear tire wouldn't go flat again, that she wouldn't take a wrong turn and end up trapped and isolated on a country road. Or run out of gas.

The white Jaguar remained in relentless pursuit, but at a distance, never moving close enough for Rhianna to see the driver or make out the license plate. She had no idea who was driving that car. No idea who had broken into her place, gone through her belongings. But the invasion of her privacy had to end. The stalking had to end.

Jumpy nerves couldn't be good for the baby. She took one hand off the steering wheel and gently massaged her swollen stomach. Two more weeks. Two more weeks until her due date. The baby kicked, and the familiar thump reassured Rhianna. She had to be strong for her baby.

Rafe Sutton's baby.

She replaced her hand on the wheel. Ignored the fear shimmying down her spine. Ignored her stomach tight against the seat belt. She resisted the urge to jam the pedal to the metal. Her old pickup wasn't up for a road race, and her reflexes weren't as good as before her pregnancy.

She wished for a cell phone or at least a CB radio to call for help, but those were luxuries this single mother-to-be couldn't afford. But her brain still worked, revving into overdrive at the danger.

While her truck sucked gas with an appetite as insatiable as a pregnant woman's, she still believed she could make another three miles.

Rhianna caught a red light. Wished she had time to check her map. She had driven to Denver on a shopping errand and didn't come here often, preferring the clean air of the mountains, the slower pace in the country and the companionship of friends and neighbors she'd known for years.

She turned right, and at the sight of a police station, let out a tense sigh. "It's okay, baby, we're going to make it."

But she'd spoken too soon. Her truck gurgled once and died. Desperate, Rhianna tried to restart the engine. But the gas gauge read empty.

One glance in the rearview mirror and her heart rate doubled. The white Jaguar had pulled over behind her. Sun glinted off the window, and she still couldn't see her pursuer.

Eight and a half months pregnant she might be, but Rhianna refused to sit like a rabbit snared in a trap. Releasing her seat belt, she opened the truck's door. And prepared to run for her life.

Chapter One

"Daniel McCloud's on the phone, Rafe. He says it's urgent."

After a moment's hesitation, Rafe Sutton nodded to the ranch hand, tossed a curry brush into a bucket and wiped his hands on a towel. "I'll be right there."

Daniel McCloud. Rhianna's father. Rafe had been trying to get her out of his mind for the last eight and a half months. Just when he'd thought he'd succeeded, her father called. Rafe hadn't talked to any of the McClouds since the night of that party. An event that came back to him now with stunning clarity.

That night, he had removed his Stetson hat, strode through the McClouds' front door and raked his hand through his hair so he didn't look as though he'd just blown in with the tumbleweeds. Even before he'd accepted a whiskey from Daniel McCloud, his host, and whetted his parched throat even as he nodded hello to several acquaintances, Rafe searched the crowded living room for a glimpse of Rhianna McCloud. He gazed over the familiar faces of the movers and shakers of the horse world, curious to see how the pesky sixteen-year-old of his memories had grown up.

A decade ago, Rhianna and her father had worked on the Sutton ranch. She'd been different from the other girls who'd been impressed with the Sutton name and fortune. She'd been coltish and slender and independent as hell. Although her teenage crush on Rafe had been unmistakable, he'd instinctively known that she'd been more interested in the way he treated his horses than in how much money they'd bring at auction. Rhianna's flirtations had flattered his twenty-two-year-old ego. But he'd never been tempted to steal a kiss; high school sophomores weren't his style.

In the decade since he'd last seen Rhianna, Rafe's tastes hadn't changed much. He typically kept company with sophisticated, slender gals who wanted a good time and no commitments. Gals who didn't cause a fuss when his roving eye moved on to the next conquest.

Rafe enjoyed the chase, the hunt, the challenge of dating. He enjoyed the feminine sex's fascinating scents, their titillating moods, their sparkling eyes when they responded to his flirtations. Yes. He enjoyed women way too much to settle on just one. In this milling crowd of horse people, he spied several interesting prospects.

Husky laughter warmed him like fine brandy and drew Rafe's gaze to the terrace. The sight of Rhianna McCloud all grown up rocked Rafe back on his spurs. The fine red hair she'd once worn in a long ponytail was now all fluffed up in long, sexy waves that looked softer than a goose-down pillow and shimmered with fire. Her strapless green dress molded her splendid curves so closely she couldn't be wearing much under it but her scent. And the animation on her face, her sheer exuberance and the pure welcome in her silky gaze as her eyes met his drew him toward her instantly.

"Rafe!" With a squeal of feminine delight, Rhianna hurried to him, flung her arms around his neck, aimed a kiss at his cheek.

As he braced himself for the impact of those lush curves against his chest and closed his arms around her, he suddenly recalled how Rhianna never hid her feelings. Never did things halfway. She blazed her own trail and lived by her own rules, refusing to let anyone trim her wings. And then other memories burst loose as her scent enveloped him in a cloud of enticing jasmine.

Grinning in delight at her enthusiastic welcome, Rafe gathered her closer and turned his head. Her lips squarely met his. Beneath his fingers, the bare, velvety flesh of her shoulders caused an unexpectedly warm tingle to scald his blood.

Rhianna pulled back, and for an instant, shock and passion clashed in her deep green eyes. Then she tilted up her chin and winked at him. Suddenly, he was no longer so sure her intentions were purely innocent.

Before Rafe regained his senses, Rhianna looped her arm through his. "Come out to the barn and I'll show you…"

Rafe licked his bottom lip, unable to resist enjoying the taste of white wine and Rhianna's vanilla-flavored lipstick. His eyes must have hinted at just what he wanted Rhianna to show him in the barn, because she swallowed hard.

Then her full lips broke into a sunny smile, her voice teasing. "I'll show you…the foal."

"Mind if we tag along?" Judge Stuart's gruff interruption helped ground Rafe's thoughts.

From the moment Rafe had heard Rhianna laugh, he'd forgotten the roomful of party goers. He'd forgotten the influential community of Colorado horse lovers who thrived on Sutton gossip and rumors as much as they did betting on the next horse race. He'd forgotten to keep his devil-may-care, laid-back attitude firmly in place, and hoped no one had noticed his lapse.

Standing beside him, Judge Stuart wore a black velvet, broomstick pleated shirt with turquoise and silver metallic rickrack. His matching black hat sported a beaded hatband, but Rafe wasn't fooled by his down home threads, knowing a brilliant mind lurked behind the impassive features. From the shrewd look in Judge Stuart's keen gaze, Rafe suspected the wily judge might have guessed just how much Rhianna's welcoming kiss had stunned him. But the judge, a friend of Rafe's father—the senior, two-term senator of Colorado—merely saluted Rafe with his glass and calmly sipped his spirits.

Janet and Hal Stone, Thoroughbred breeders and Rafe's main competition for prime horseflesh, weren't as discreet. Janet gazed from Rhianna to Rafe, her golden eyes brimming with mischief. "I'm sorry I missed your brother Cameron's wedding. But perhaps next time, we'll be in the States."

The Stones' passion for travel sent them on frequent jaunts to Europe, Asia and South America. They might have missed the latest Sutton wedding, but they invariably showed their faces whenever good horseflesh came on the market.

Hal Stone, a distinguished, gray-haired rancher, always went in for a lot of fancy rigging. Cocky as the king of spades, he set his own style and wore an Armani suit with a diamond belt buckle and monogrammed boots. Not to be outdone, his wife wore a black blouse with lacy sleeves over a lacy black brassiere, a hot pink neckerchief that matched her pink suede boots, and poured-on designer jeans.

Hal shook Rafe's hand and gave him a friendly nod. "The senator sure knows how to throw a wedding. Any chance he'll have another one soon?"

Hal's question might have been ambiguous, but his meaning was explicit. He clearly wanted to know if Rafe intended to marry Rhianna. Had everyone in the damn room seen their kiss? And drawn the wrong conclusions…?

Rafe gave away none of his annoyance at himself for being caught like a schoolboy. Long practiced in avoiding probing questions, he shrugged lightly. "Couldn't tell you." Then he turned to Janet and kissed her lightly on the cheek, knowing his gesture would irritate Hal, who adored his beautiful young wife and jealously guarded her from other men. Served him right for marrying a woman half his age. Although Rafe had to admit that Janet looked glowingly happy, and the pair seemed well suited. Content.

But not every loving couple led such charmed lives. Rafe had watched his father lose his mother. Seen how devastated his brother Cameron had been after the murder of his first wife. Rafe preferred to take lovely women where he found them and then leave them with happy memories.

Rhianna had remained silent during the brief exchanges, but she hadn't removed her arm from his. She seemed satisfied to stare at him fondly and let him make the next move. Before Rafe could decide exactly what that move should be, their group grew again.

Duncan Phillips, a wealthy horse breeder with a nearby ranch, shook hands with the judge, Hal and Rafe, then bowed to the women, greeting them with genteel European manners that matched his impeccably cut suit, before announcing his real reason for coming over. "Did someone mention a visit to the wonder horse?"

At Duncan's appearance, Rhianna held her head higher and leaned just a bit tighter against Rafe's side. "The foal's name is Sweetness."

"Silly name for a stallion," Duncan scoffed, without much heat.

"You buy him and you can change his name," Judge Stuart muttered.

Rhianna kept her tone light. "Sweetness isn't for sale."

Hal frowned. "Isn't this party to whet our interest?"

"And up the asking price?" Janet added.

"Exactly right," Duncan answered, as if he already owned the foal.

Rhianna's casual demeanor stiffened ever so slightly, and Rafe wouldn't have noticed the tension radiating through her if he hadn't been so attuned to her every movement. If she needed protection from Duncan's sharp tongue, Rafe would oblige. If she wanted to make the handsome millionaire jealous, Rafe could help there, too. He slipped his arm from her elbow, slung it proprietarily over her shoulders and drew her even closer.

She snuggled against him like a warm puppy. "Duncan, I'm afraid this is just one of those *rare* times when you're wrong. This party is a celebration over the McClouds' good fortune—nothing more. We intend to raise Sweetness ourselves and race him as a two-year-old."

Duncan adjusted his cuff link and eyed Rhianna with bitterness. "*Good fortune* is what you're calling Destiny, the winningest stallion in history, breaking out of his stall and breeding with your mare?"

Janet Stone frowned at Duncan. "Are you saying Destiny *didn't* leap out of his stall at your ranch when Rhianna stopped by to visit?"

Duncan shrugged, raising his voice so everyone in the room could hear his accusation. "Isn't it convenient that Rhianna's mare just happened to go into heat?"

Rhianna kept her tone light. "Mares can be unpredictable that way."

"And isn't it convenient that Rhianna left the mare in a stall near Destiny, a champion of the Kentucky Derby, the Preakness and the Belmont Stakes?"

"As if I knew you'd brought him home." Rhianna rolled her eyes at the ceiling, but Rafe could feel the tension radiating from her in heated waves. The old Rhianna would have jabbed the man in the jaw, and

Rafe was surprised to discover she'd learned to control her temper.

Duncan was an idiot. If he couldn't control his stallion, he had no right to claim a stud fee or to blame Rhianna when nature took its natural course between a randy stallion and a mare in heat.

Rhianna glared at Duncan, but Rafe felt her trembling with rage. "I placed my mare in the same stall I'd used before. I had no idea the stallion was a mere two doors down. And you know why I came by. To end our relationship."

"And steal a stud fee you couldn't afford to purchase."

At Duncan's nasty insinuation, Rhianna grabbed Duncan's drink from his hand and tossed it into his face. Now this was the Rhianna Rafe remembered. Proud. Courageous. Refusing to let any man cow her with insults.

The arrogant horse breeder mopped his sopping face with a handkerchief, his skin red with anger and humiliation. As Duncan sputtered in indignation, Rafe restrained a grin. "I believe you owe the lady an apology."

The muscles in Duncan's neck bulged as he pointed his finger in Rhianna's face. "I'll apologize just as soon as she pays my stud fee."

Rhianna shoved his hand away. "If you have to rely on money for what *you* offer, then you're not going to be rich for long."

Rafe stepped between Rhianna and Duncan. He kept his voice low, his arms loose and ready for action, though whether in preparation to deck Duncan or keep Rhianna from doing so, he wasn't sure.

"What's the matter, Duncan? Are you hurting so badly for cash? Or did the lady hurt your feelings when she dumped you?"

"She used me."

Rhianna tried to step around Rafe. "Bull! Did I take your ruby necklace? Did I accept your fancy engagement ring?"

Janet gasped. "Duncan asked you to marry him?"

Duncan stuffed his wet handkerchief into his pocket, stomped away and muttered loudly enough for half the roomful of guests to hear, "I should have known she didn't have enough sense to realize how lucky she was. Imagine turning me down."

Hal shook his head. "Good riddance."

"Here, here." Judge Stuart patted Rhianna on the shoulder. "You can do better. Much better. Now, don't you have a horse to show us?"

Rafe took Rhianna's hand as she led the group outside to the barn. Another woman might have burst into tears after the ugly scene. Rhianna kept her head high, her spine straight, but she clutched Rafe's hand so hard he couldn't mistake her fury.

Daniel McCloud kept the barn immaculate. The scent of fresh hay greeted them, along with soft nickers and welcoming snorts.

Rhianna proudly led Janet, Hal, Judge Stuart and Rafe to the two-week-old foal. And for the second time that evening, Rafe's appetite spiraled, his hunger whetted. The chestnut Thoroughbred boasted spectacularly long legs, and Rafe would bet he'd grow to a full seventeen hands high. But it wasn't just the general characteristics that interested Rafe; well-laid back shoulders, an elegant neck, a short, strong body deep through the girth, well-muscled quarters and clean hard legs. The foal's head captured his imagination and caused him to envision winners' circles. With his proud bearing, Sweetness gave an impression of quality, refinement and intelligence, a grand nobility.

The foal nuzzled Rhianna, and she scratched behind his ears, her face softening. "Dad likes the foals to become used to people at birth. Sweetness enjoys his grooming. He's a friendly little guy."

Janet lifted her hand for the foal to become accustomed to her scent. "He's gorgeous. You sure you don't want to sell him?"

Rhianna shook her head.

"Can you afford to stable him?" Hal asked. "The feed and veterinarian bills will be astronomical."

"We'll manage. Somehow."

Raising a racehorse was an expensive proposition. But the payoffs could be spectacular. Although it would be years before the McClouds would put Sweetness up for stud, Rafe was already imagining crossing the foal's bloodlines with several of his mares. Deep in thought, he studied the foal. Something about the horse almost shouted "Champion." He already had a special rhythm in his gait. A certain undaunted flick of his ears, as if he knew he was fast. And the spirit in his eyes told Rafe that this animal had Winner stamped all over him.

Rhianna's hand on Rafe's shoulder brought him back to reality. He'd been studying the horse so hard he hadn't even noticed when the others had left. "He's spectacular," Rafe admitted.

"Thank you." Rhianna slid her arms around him, and she fitted against him just right. For a moment he wondered why he'd always preferred thin, small-breasted women when he could have gone for a woman with curves. And then Rhianna's lips met his, but not before he saw the aftereffects of Duncan's hurtful words still clouding her lovely eyes.

Surprised by her action, he kissed her gently, then pushed her away. "Rhianna, what's this about?"

Her brows arched over wide, green eyes. "Isn't it obvious? I'm not a child anymore, Rafe."

"That's more than obvious. You've changed. I haven't."

She kissed his neck, and a tremor rocked him. "So, you're still one of those love 'em and leave 'em kind of men."

He didn't deny the truth, but cocked an eyebrow. "And that doesn't bother you?" This grown-up Rhianna was just full of surprises, and he was having difficulty adjusting to the new version.

"When I was sixteen, I had a crush on you. I wanted to cut off your dates' hair—each and every one of them."

"You're not sixteen anymore." Rafe fisted his hands into her hair, gorgeous red locks that shimmered like an autumn sunset. He marveled at the softness until he revealed her delicate neckline, where he traced a path to her collarbone with his lips.

"Precisely my point. There's a lot you don't know about me," she murmured.

"I'm willing to learn." He reached for the zipper at her back, amazed that his hand trembled. Years ago, she'd been like a pesky kid sister to him. He'd never thought of Rhianna this way—as a woman, a woman with needs and wants and desires beyond her horses. Now he wanted her badly, with a hunger he hadn't known in a long time. Maybe ever. She smelled so good, felt so right, and the fire she'd kindled with her first kiss flared again.

He'd always suspected Rhianna McCloud would grow into a fascinating woman. But he'd never imagined she could be so eager, so passionate, so willing. He hadn't specifically kept track of her, but the horse set was its own small world, and her father was one of the best trainers in the country.

Though she was known for her warmth and genuineness, when it came to dating, Rhianna had the reputation of a cautious woman. As far as he knew, she'd only been serious with one man. She'd never been free with her favors, preferring to spend her time with the horses rather than with the boys who used to hang around the Sutton barn.

She tugged him closer and whispered into his mouth. "There's a blanket in the hayloft. I read up there sometimes."

Her invitation was so clear, he almost kicked out of his boots. "You want to show me…your library?"

"I intend to show you much more than my library." At the suggestive huskiness in her tone, Rafe's jaw must have dropped. She started toward the ladder and spoke over her shoulder. "I'm a big girl. I know what I want."

She wanted him.

Amazed, excited and still in shock, Rafe couldn't get over the changes in her. Rhianna knew his reputation. She knew he never spent more than a few weeks with a lady before moving on. Rhianna and he went way back. He didn't want to hurt her or lead her to believe anything could come from a romp in the hayloft except one night of pleasure.

He stepped to the ladder, enjoyed the sight of her kicking off her shoes and tossing them above. Agile as a cat, she climbed, and he followed her up the ladder into the hayloft, where he spied a reading lamp, a bookcase stacked with books, chocolates and fresh daisies in a jar. She tossed a blanket over a bed of hay, then dragged him down beside her. "Now all we need is rain."

"Rain?"

"It's romantic, don't you think? All that power of nature unleashed while we're safe and cozy. Besides, I like the sound of raindrops on tin."

In some ways she appeared the most sophisticated of women. Yet she could enjoy simple pleasures, and that made him want her all the more. Rhianna the schoolgirl had charmed him. Rhianna the woman set a fire burning in him that smoldered with intensity and promise.

Rafe tumbled onto the blanket beside her, already knowing the night would be special. The air tasted sweeter just from Rhianna's presence. The weather even cooperated, as lightning lit up the night sky and thunder rolled across the mountains. Light rain pattered on the tin roof, enclosing them in their own private cocoon.

With Rhianna's auburn hair cascading onto the blanket, a perfect foil for her wide eyes, dark as an evergreen forest, he had to take a deep breath and remind himself of the pleasure to be gained by going slowly. But he could barely contain his impatience as he marveled at the avid light in her eyes and the kind of curves a man could only dream about.

She reached for his shirt and unfastened the first three buttons before he slipped down to her toes. He nibbled the inside of the arch of one foot, caressed her delicate ankle, wanting to leave no part of her untouched.

"That tickles," she murmured.

"You have pretty feet."

She sat up and eyed him suspiciously. "Rafe Sutton, you don't have a foot fetish, do you?"

"I'm just deciding which part of you I like the best."

"Oh."

"And until I investigate all of you—"

"Hmm. I like the sound of that."

He trailed his hand up her calf and played with a delicate spot behind her knee, tracing lazy circles. "My investigation could take hours."

"Hours?"

Rafe sensed her inexperience behind her sassy impatience, and set out to put her mind at ease. "Relax, sweetheart. We won't do anything you don't like."

She threaded her fingers through his hair, her voice throaty with a hint of excitement and desire. "I think I'd like to try everything once."

"That's the Rhianna I remember." He shimmied up from her knees to look her in the eye. Up close her eyes were a clear, luminous green surrounded by a glittering circle of dark emerald. "You were always fearless."

She sighed as she nipped his shoulder. "And you always had a silver tongue."

He kissed her deeply and wondered if he should stop. This was no ordinary seduction—not for him. Too many feelings surged through him, mucking up his thoughts and making him unsure of himself. Rhianna's pure uninhibited pleasure, her complete submission to her own desires and his, had Rafe edgy. His pulse kicked hard. This union would be much more than shared pleasure and simple release.

He should apologize to the lady and get the hell out. But he couldn't. And he couldn't deny her, any more than he could deny himself the exquisite bliss of discovering how good lovemaking could be.

He would give himself the night, one night of bliss. One night to savor this special woman. Surely a man couldn't fall in love in just one night?

Chapter Two

And Rafe hadn't fallen in love, he assured himself. Although making love to Rhianna had been special, it was so special he never intended to do it again. He refused to be caught in that trap. But if he was really a love 'em and leave 'em kind of guy, why did his attraction to Rhianna scare him so much? He'd proved he could stay away from Rhianna for the past eight and a half months, refusing to phone her, using any excuse to stay out of the Denver area. After all this time had passed, he thought it odd that McCloud would call. The foal hadn't raced yet, and Sweetness was still too young for stud. Perhaps the foal had taken ill and needed Rafe's new vet?

Rafe hurried from the barn to the house he'd built on Sutton land. After Brent's murder, his father had deeded each of his four sons a huge tract of acreage, but the brothers still ran the ranch as one big operation—or Tyler, the eldest brother, did. Chase, the next eldest, divided his time between the Sutton operation and his wife's ranch at the Embry place, while Cameron had set up a medical practice in Highview.

The current arrangement suited Rafe just fine. His

brothers had left him free to rebuild the stable. He'd begun by erecting a new barn, since the old one had burned to the ground last year. He kept a veterinarian on permanent call, had hired a trainer, and then, educating himself about breeding stock, had set out acquiring the best of the best. Slowly, surely, Rafe built a reputation that had spread within the state and then coast to coast. Other breeders and trainers often called for his opinions and advice.

Rafe entered his house and reminded himself once again that if he'd remember to carry his cell phone with him, he would have to do less commuting between the barn and his house. Only he hated interruptions while working with his animals.

With a sigh, he tossed his hat on a peg and picked up the phone. "How are you, Daniel?"

"Fine."

"The foal coming along?"

"That's why I called."

Rafe's pulse edged up a notch. There was nothing worse than a prime animal coming down with the croup or pulling up lame. And Sweetness was born to run...just like Rhianna was born to love.

Damn.

That thought about Rhianna had sneaked in when he wasn't paying attention. The woman might be easy on the eyes, but she sure was brutal on the heart. Why couldn't he forget her?

McCloud cleared his throat. "You still want to buy the foal?"

Rafe didn't hesitate a second. "Yes, sir."

But why was McCloud willing to sell him? He must need the money badly, and for a moment Rafe felt sympathy for the man who would have to forfeit such a magnificent animal. But business was business. Daniel McCloud's loss could be Rafe Sutton's gain.

And what an addition to the Sutton stable Sweetness would be. Even if the foal's speed didn't pan out, Rafe wanted to mix those championship bloodlines with several of his mares. The stud fees alone would make him worth any reasonable price.

"How much do you want for him?"

McCloud named a price that Rafe found agreeable. "You've got a deal."

But then McCloud added, "There's just one condition."

A condition? That McCloud wanted to dictate terms was highly unusual. But then so was the horse. Rafe imagined the trainer wanted to arrange for a stud with another of his own mares in a year or so, and that would be acceptable.

"I'll only sell him to you if you help out Rhianna."

"Rhianna?" Surprise turned Rafe's nerves edgy.

"She's in a bit of trouble."

"Trouble?" Rafe shut his mouth, realizing he was starting to sound like a parrot. He just couldn't imagine Rhianna in trouble. Or why Daniel had come to him.

"It might take some of your lawyering skills. I'm not sure."

Rafe propped his boots on his desk and leaned back in his chair, but his casual pose did nothing to relieve the sudden pressure in his chest. He'd attended law school to please his father and to have a career to fall back on in case he didn't succeed as a horse breeder. If Rhianna was in trouble, she should have the benefit of a more experienced attorney than Rafe. "Look, I've got a law degree, but I'm not a practicing attorney. You'd be better off selling me the horse and hiring—"

"No."

No?

Rafe took a deep breath, trying to clear his head, trying to think straight, but when it came to Rhianna that wasn't easy. He could still remember how she felt, how she tasted, how she'd spoiled his desire for any other woman. Hell, maybe he needed to see her again to get her out of his system.

Daniel's offer of Sweetness made Rafe realize that he would never have made such an offer unless Rhianna was in real trouble. And while Rafe might make a business deal if Daniel needed money, Rafe wouldn't profit off Rhianna's trouble.

Rafe considered Rhianna a friend and he would help without being bribed by the offer of a horse. Gripping the phone tighter, Rafe set about straightening out Daniel.

"If Rhianna needs my help, she has it. I can't buy Sweetness under these circumstances."

"And I don't take charity," Daniel countered.

Rafe heard the pride in the man's voice and decided Rhianna's well-being was more important than arguing with her father.

Rafe thrummed his fingers on the desk. "Daniel, why don't you start at the beginning and explain what kind of trouble she's in."

"We're not exactly sure, but we think she's being stalked by some psycho."

The pressure in Rafe's chest increased with worry. "Have you gone to the police?"

"They can't guard her twenty-four hours a day."

Rhianna needed round-the-clock protection from some nutcase, and her father wanted *him?* Why him? Rafe frowned, still puzzled. "You want me to protect her? Why not hire a bodyguard?"

"Look, I think it would be better if Rhianna explained everything to you in person."

Daniel McCloud was trying to suck Rafe in. And it was working. Rafe tried to tell himself he would go to Rhianna and help her because he was worried over her safety. But he refused to lie to himself. Yes, he was worried. But he also wanted to see Rhianna. He didn't like the thought of some madman stalking her, and realized that McCloud must be at his wit's end to make him the offer. The man must be fearful for his daughter's life.

A sudden chill on Rafe's neck erased all his hesitation. He checked his watch and calculated the time. "I'll be in the Denver area by late afternoon."

RHIANNA MCCLOUD LOOKED UP and down the Denver street, praying for a black-and-white squad car. Where were the police when you needed them?

With no help in sight, she grabbed her keys, her purse and the gun she kept loaded in the glove compartment. She'd shoot the stalker if necessary and be grateful that her mother had insisted she learn to defend herself. Still, Rhianna knew the danger of using force. In her condition, she moved slowly. If she fired the gun and missed, the weapon could be turned against her. And her unborn child.

Rhianna couldn't waste a precious second—not with the stalker so close. She scooted out of the truck. Headed for the police station.

She heard her pursuer slam his car door. Heard footsteps behind her.

Rhianna clutched the gun. At this stage of her pregnancy, a fast waddle was all she could muster. Gritting her teeth, she hurried on.

The footsteps behind her grew louder, and her pulse skyrocketed.

A hand clamped down on her shoulder.

Rhianna spun, raised the gun and pointed. "Don't touch me!"

"And hello to..."

Rafe Sutton's words died in his throat as he stared at her, wide-eyed. Not from fear of the gun she'd pointed at his heart, but at the sight of her swollen belly. "You're pregnant?"

"Duh." Rhianna put the gun away in her pocket. "Why the hell are you following me?"

"You're having a baby?"

Rafe sounded so surprised Rhianna instinctively knew he couldn't be her stalker. But she kept her mental defenses up—unsure why she felt as if she still needed to protect herself.

Damn him. He looked as handsome as ever, tall, dark haired and gray eyed like all the Suttons. But unlike his brothers, Rafe moved like a cat, with a natural grace and balance that most bronc busters would trade their best boots for.

He was whipcord lean, while she was as fat as a cow. His quicksilver eyes darkened with shadows. She didn't like him seeing her like this. And then she remembered how he'd treated her. Not even one phone call in eight and half months. He hadn't cared enough about her when she'd been thin to even pen a note. Even worse, he'd proved he had no feelings for her—so she had no time for him now.

She gestured with her hand, determined not to let a speck of pain or uncertainty or anger flicker in her eyes. "Go away."

Passersby walked around them. No one seemed to notice her panic. Rafe ignored her request for him to leave. He stood mute on the sidewalk, counting on his fingers. Counting months? With her stomach so large, she looked ready to deliver and he could easily guess she was nine months pregnant.

His eyes turned to smoke. "The baby's mine," he drawled in a nonthreatening manner, as if he feared she would refuse to confirm his words.

She had to give him credit. They'd used a condom. He could have salvaged his conscience, done the easy thing and walked away. Just assumed the baby wasn't his. Assumed the child was another man's. Her heart softened toward him because he hadn't even asked.

But Rafe Sutton didn't take the easy way out. He might be shocked by her condition, he might be livid that she'd kept the baby, but he would know the truth.

She held his gaze. "I was going to tell you—"

"When?" He snapped the word like a whip, his voice turning to flint. He looked dark, dangerous and threateningly male.

"After he or she was born."

"I'm supposed to believe you?"

At the distrust in his tone, her heart turned hard as granite. "I don't give a rat's ass what you believe.

But I would have told you. Not for your sake, but for our baby's.''

"You need money?''

She wanted to slap him, but knew she'd only hurt her hand on those chiseled cheeks. Ignoring his insult, she kept her tone even, knowing the effort would cost her tears in her pillow tonight. "I think a child has the right to know who his father is.''

"I'm sorry. I shouldn't have said that.'' He sounded sincere, but she was in no mood to forgive him. Not when her feet hurt. Not when she had to pee every twenty minutes. Not when her hormones were raging in fear for her life.

As if sensing her need to rest, he led her to a sidewalk bench, and she sat, grateful to take the weight off her swollen feet, but apprehensive about the coming conversation. All around them the world moved on. A squirrel stashed an acorn in its cheek. Traffic rushed by and mothers pushed baby strollers down the sidewalk.

Rhianna's world had just turned upside down. She'd dreaded this moment for months. And now that it had arrived, she wanted to say the right thing, make Rafe understand the choices she'd made, so he could go on with his life and she could do the same.

She had the impression Rafe had already adjusted to the fact that he would be a daddy, and didn't mind too much. But she couldn't be sure. Maybe he was in shock. Rafe had always been hard to read, hiding his emotions behind an easygoing personality. The fact that he'd snapped at her revealed how shaken he really was.

Rafe looked at her stomach and then away. "Why

didn't you call as soon as you knew?'' he asked, sounding puzzled and almost hurt.

Hurt? How could he be hurt? And why couldn't he figure out the obvious for himself?

She blew a strand of hair out of her face in exasperation. ''Why didn't I tell you? Because I was hoping you would come back, despite our argument the next morning.''

Rhianna would never forget their parting words. He'd tried to leave without her knowing, but she'd awakened. She'd been angry that he'd tried to sneak out without saying goodbye. Hurt that he hadn't realized just how special the night had been, and hurt that he was willing to throw it all away in exchange for his precious freedom. Hurt and upset and not quite awake, she'd sarcastically asked if he'd spent the *entire* night with her trying to soften her up so she'd sell him the foal. At her accusation, he'd been insulted and had stalked out. And she hadn't heard from him since.

She'd known this confrontation was coming, and she'd hoped to put it off longer. But she'd tell him the truth—even if she knew he didn't really want to hear it. ''I was hoping you'd come back for *me*—not out of duty to our child.'' He flinched at her direct reply, but she didn't care if he felt guilty. ''When I learned I was pregnant, I was shocked but happy. My first impulse was to call you and tell you.''

''But you didn't.''

''I was reluctant for several reasons.''

''What reasons could you have to hide your pregnancy from me? Don't you think I had a right to know?'' His voice remained soft, but the unmistakable edge of steel beneath told her that although he might listen to her side, he disagreed with her decision.

Of course she'd thought he had a right to know. But she'd been fearful on many levels. She still was. "I was afraid you might think I planned the pregnancy to force you into marriage."

He looked genuinely puzzled. "We used protection. How could I blame you?"

She shrugged. "I was even more worried you'd try and take the baby away from me. My family can't afford a court battle and high legal fees."

"You think I'd separate a mother and her child?"

"Would you?" She searched his eyes, and he was the first to look away.

"I don't know."

At his reply, fear spiked down her spine. She'd always known Rafe sure as hell didn't want to get married. But it wasn't his way to be cruel. Nor did she believe he would deliberately try to make things harder for her than they already were.

The baby kicked, and absently she massaged her swollen belly.

Rafe's eyes widened. "Are you having contractions?"

"Not yet. I'm not due for another two weeks. That was just a kick."

Rafe watched her rub the spot, then glanced away as if embarrassed to have been caught looking.

Without thinking, Rhianna took his hand and placed it on her belly. "Feel."

As the baby kicked, Rafe looked proud and very male, and Rhianna realized that she'd made a mistake.

She didn't want Rafe to think about being a father. She didn't want him to think of this baby as his.

But it was too late. He had a smug gleam in his eyes, and his lips had softened. "She's strong."

"She?"

"You're carrying high. She's a girl."

"That's an old wives' tale."

"How do you think old wives' tales get passed down from one generation to another? Because they're based on fact." Rafe kept Rhianna's hand and turned to face her more directly. "I don't take my responsibilities lightly. I know what it's like to grow up with only one parent. My mother died when I was just a kid." He said the words without feeling, and that lack of emotion revealed just how much pain the loss had caused him. "I don't want that for my child—"

"*Your* child?" Fear clutched her heart. The Suttons were a powerful, wealthy family. If it came down to a custody fight, her parents would do everything in their power to support her. But they were already two months behind on the foal's feed bill, and her truck was in desperate need of repairs that they couldn't afford.

"*Our* child. And you had no right to make that decision for her by yourself."

"I'd hoped…"

"Hoped what?"

"That we could work things out somehow." She twisted her hands in her lap, knowing that despite her anger toward Rafe for abandoning her the last eight and a half months, she had to rein in her temper and work this out like an adult. "I've never regretted the night we spent together. I made love to you with my eyes wide-open. I knew you didn't want commitments.''

She couldn't disguise the cutting pain in her voice, and realized she was being too honest with him. But that was her way. Rhianna was always honest about her feelings, and if that made him feel even more guilty, too damn bad.

She'd hoped for more from him now. Rhianna reminded herself she'd had months and months to think things through. Rafe had had less than an hour. She'd thrown so many surprises at him that he needed time to digest the news.

Yet she wanted him gone, the issue settled. Just looking at him caused anxiety and longings and stress that couldn't be good for the baby.

She raised her chin and looked him square in the eyes. "I don't need you, Rafe. Not your money. Not your name. I'll manage. The baby will be well cared for.''

''That's not the point.''

She scratched her neck. "Am I missing something? You didn't want me. You don't want our baby, so I'll take care of it.'' She shooed him away. "Go back to your ranch and your horses. We'll be fine. I can support the baby myself. My mother is more than willing to provide child care while I work. Dad can give the baby a stable male influence in its life. Our baby will have plenty of love. You can walk away with a clear conscience.''

His face hardened to stone. "Sure. I'll just walk away. Abandon a woman who's pregnant with my child. A woman who thinks nothing of putting that baby's life in danger. You weren't going to tell me about the stalker?''

She bit her lip to keep back her gasp of dismay. Now that his protective instincts were on alert, she knew he'd never walk away. He'd feel obligated to help her, become accustomed to the idea of being a father, grow to love the child. And take it away from her. Her heart pounded, wild with worry. She mustn't let her fears run away with her. She had to stay in control.

She fought to keep her tone calm. ''How did you hear?''

Rafe's eyes narrowed. ''Daniel called me. He's worried about your safety—even if you aren't.''

''I've taken precautions.''

''Really?''

She patted the gun in her pocket. ''We'll be fine. Right now I'm more worried about finding a bathroom than avoiding the stalker.''

He took her arm and gently helped her to her feet. ''That shows you have no judgment.''

She sighed. ''You wouldn't say that if the baby's head was pressing against *your* bladder.''

RAFE WAS GOING TO BE a father. In two weeks. If Daniel McCloud hadn't called, he might not have found out about the baby in time to help Rhianna.

As Rafe waited at a restaurant table for Rhianna to use the rest room, he made a few arrangements on his cell phone while he tried to wrap his mind around the idea of fatherhood. He should think about dirty diapers, the terrible twos, Friday and Saturday night activities curtailed. But Rafe had had the joy of baby-sitting his nephew Keith, and Cameron's twins. He knew the warmth of little ones' smiles, the sunshine of their laughter, the way an adult suddenly saw the world through the wondrous new eyes of a child.

Although he would make sure Rhianna had no money worries, could he walk away and allow her to raise his offspring? He had no doubt she would be an excellent mother. She had a good head on her shoulders. A good heart. A loving family.

She'd given him a way out. Why couldn't he take it? Why did his conscience nag him like a stubborn mule? Perhaps it was merely her safety that concerned him, but he refused to use such an easy excuse. His feelings were way more complex than that.

No closer to resolving the issue by the time Rhianna returned, he watched her walk toward him. He didn't see the glowing skin or shining happiness in her eyes that he remembered with his sister-in-law's second pregnancy. Rhianna looked wary, guarded. Dusky circles under her eyes revealed she hadn't been sleeping well. Yet to Rafe she looked beautiful. Her huge belly carried his child, and he couldn't suppress the swell of pride that rose in his chest.

Rhianna took the seat opposite him. "Have you ordered yet?"

"Just coffee. Are you hungry?"

"I'm always hungry." She picked up a menu with the first genuine grin he'd seen that morning. Her entire face lit up, and his heart clenched at the strain she'd been carrying alone.

She licked her lush bottom lip as she looked over the menu. He recalled those lips on his, on his throat, teasing his ear. What the hell was wrong with him? For God's sake, the woman was eight and a half months pregnant and he was lusting after her like a man starved for sex—which wasn't far from the truth. Rhianna had spoiled other women for him. And now he would pay the price. Luckily the tabletop hid his jeans, which had grown uncomfortably tight.

"Order whatever you like."

She grinned again. "You shouldn't have said that." The waitress approached and Rhianna ordered. "I'd like the Belgian waffles with whipped cream and strawberries, two eggs over easy, two slices of bacon—crisp please—two English muffins lightly toasted. A large glass of orange juice and another glass of ice. Oh, and a glass of milk, too."

"Coming right up." The waitress turned away.

Rhianna called her back. "Miss."

"Yes?"

"Aren't you going to ask what he'd like?"

"Sorry, ma'am. I just assumed you'd ordered for both of you."

Rhianna patted her stomach. "I did. For me and the baby."

Rafe gave the waitress his order and then gazed at Rhianna. "Tell me about the stalker."

Rhianna frowned. "You sure know how to spoil a meal. What did Dad tell you?"

"He said it would be better if you explained."

"And you came because…"

Rafe hesitated. "I came because I was worried."

If Rhianna was in danger, then his child was in danger.

Suttons protected their own.

Luckily, the waitress delivered her orange juice and English muffins, distracting Rhianna. She slathered butter and then jelly on the muffins, and Rafe marveled that she hadn't gained fifty pounds. Her stomach might be enormous, but her face and arms remained thin as fence rails. Obviously the baby needed whatever she was feeding it.

She poured half the orange juice into the glass filled with ice. "You get more juice this way," she explained. "Otherwise the ice takes up half the glass."

Talking between sips of juice and delicate bites of the muffin, she told him her troubles. "It started with a car that followed me around town. And it's happened several times. The car never comes close enough for me to see the license plates or the driver. When I spotted you in my rearview mirror, I drove to the police station. Why were you following me?"

"To see if anyone was following you. I never dreamed you'd think I was the stalker." Rafe frowned, recalling the police station two blocks away. "Why'd you park so far away?"

She shrugged sheepishly. "I ran out of gas."

"Go on."

"I reported the stalker to the police. They thought I was delusional—due to my pregnancy. But I know what I saw."

"The car never comes close to you?"

"Nope."

"What make and color was it?"

"It changed almost every time."

Rafe scratched his head, wondering if the police were correct about her state of mind. But he knew

Rhianna better than that. She wasn't prone to panic. He'd once seen her calm a horse that had gone ballistic after a bee sting. She'd kept her head, kept the horse from injuring himself.

"Then what happened?"

"Six months ago someone let the air out of all four of my truck's tires. I thought it might be a kid's prank."

The waitress delivered her bacon and eggs and his omelette. "I'm saving your waffles for dessert, hon. I wouldn't want them to get cold."

"Thanks." Rhianna held out her empty glass. "More milk, please."

Rafe wondered where she put it all, but even a bachelor like him knew better than to comment about a hungry, pregnant woman and her food. "When did you start carrying the gun?"

Rhianna paused between bites, her eyes haunted by the memory. "My bedroom's in the back of the house. I have my own entrance. While I was at work, someone entered my room, and…they moved things."

"Nothing was taken?"

She shook her head.

"You're sure things were moved."

"Very." She licked a dab of butter off the tip of her thumb. A very delectable thumb that he'd like to explore with his own tongue.

Down, boy. He had to force his thoughts to stay on her story.

"My underwear was laid out on the bed, where it would have been if I'd been lying there, wearing it."

At her reluctance to speak, he sensed there was more. "Go on."

"A knife stuck out of my bloody pillow."

"Bloody?"

"The police said he used chicken blood."

A chill went down Rafe's spine. This was the work of a sick mind. "I'm sorry. Did the police—"

"—check for prints?" She stopped eating for another moment. "They dusted the entire room. Didn't find a thing. Said the perpetrator must have worn gloves. The lock wasn't even forced."

"So why don't the police believe you?"

"They think I did it for attention. Who would want that kind of attention?"

Rafe didn't want to pry, didn't want to know, but necessity made him ask, "Did you give anyone a key?"

She sighed and continued to eat. "That would have been too easy. I've never given anyone a key. And my door is keyed the same as the front door, but only my room was disturbed."

Disturbed? Talk about understating a horrifying moment. She had to have been terrified. Another woman might have come running to him for help. Apparently Rhianna hadn't even considered him an option. Strangely, that hurt.

Rhianna had just polished off her bacon when the waitress returned with her milk and waffles. Rafe couldn't eat another bite after the story she'd told him. His stomach churned with worry.

"So I started carrying the gun. I do know how to use it."

"Could you shoot someone?" he asked gently.

Rhianna suddenly shoved away from the table, stood and headed toward the rest room. ''Be back in a minute.''

Rafe hadn't realized the inconvenience of pregnancy, hadn't ever thought about it except in regards to horses and cows. He'd delivered calves and foals since he was a kid. As familiar as he was with animals breeding, Rhianna's pregnancy was different. He couldn't help but worry that the stress of the stalker might be affecting the baby's health.

And he now understood why Daniel McCloud had called him. McCloud was no fool. Her father had called him because Rafe had a personal stake in Rhianna's safety. While Rhianna still lived with her parents, Daniel had to work. Her father couldn't afford to stay with Rhianna and protect her twenty-four hours a day. Knowing Rhianna's stubbornness, she probably hadn't told Daniel that Rafe was the father. But once McCloud had learned of Rhianna's pregnancy, he could count backward to the night of the party as well as anyone. Rafe and Rhianna had disappeared for the evening, making it easy to figure out that Rafe was the baby's father.

Rhianna had spent eight and a half months alone. Rafe would be damned if he'd let her face this stalker for another day by herself. He would protect her and the baby to the best of his ability. Now all he had to do was convince Rhianna to let him.

Rafe paid the check and glanced anxiously toward the rest room. Unlike Rhianna's first trip there, this one was taking a long time. Rafe waited another two minutes, then walked to the ladies' room and knocked lightly. When Rhianna didn't answer, he opened the door.

"Rhianna. You all right?"

No one answered.

Puzzled and worried she'd taken ill, Rafe stepped inside the small bathroom.

She was gone.

Chapter Three

Fear poured over Rafe like an icy shower. Where was Rhianna? Had the stalker followed them to the restaurant? Had he and Rhianna been too busy discussing their personal problems to notice a suspicious character lurking nearby?

The bathroom window was too small to make an escape. And Rafe would have noticed if Rhianna had gone out the front. Spinning on his heel, Rafe turned and opened a door marked Office.

Empty.

Turning down a narrow hallway, he broke into a sweat. He burst through a door marked Exit, and found himself in an alley. He looked right.

Nothing.

He looked left. His breath went out with a whoosh of relief. Rhianna stood against a wall. Alone.

As he strode toward her, he wondered if the relief he felt had come too soon. She didn't look well. Her face had lost all color, and her eyes glittered like a horse caught in truck headlights. She didn't so much as turn her head as he approached, didn't twitch a muscle, as if she were focused inward and oblivious to the world.

He eased a hand under her elbow. "What's wrong?"

"I needed some air." Her words came without inflection, from a distance.

"Are you in pain?"

"Just a little dizzy."

Prepared to catch her if necessary, Rafe slid his arm around her waist. "Lean on me and breathe deeply. You shouldn't be out here alone."

"Stuff it." Her words were weak, the will behind them strong.

"Excuse me?" Rafe wondered just what he had done or said to irritate her. He thought he was being kind and reasonable. Protective.

"Don't tell me what to do." She closed her eyes wearily. "Can't you just give me a minute?"

"Sure." He'd give her whatever she needed, but he doubted she wanted to hear that. Even weak and dizzy, Rhianna had too much stubborn pride to admit to needing anyone. Especially him. He'd hurt her by ignoring her for months, and he couldn't reasonably expect her to easily forgive him.

"Don't patronize me, Rafe. I've had dizzy spells for months. It's nothing to worry about, just my low blood pressure." She breathed in through her nose, out through her mouth. Slowly her color returned to normal, and she opened her eyes. "I know how to deal with it. See? And I'm sorry I snapped at you. It seems as though everyone is either giving me advice, hovering or asking if I'm in labor. Just because I'm carrying a baby doesn't mean I'm helpless, or that my brain's quit working. It gets old after a while. And reining in my temper was never my strong suit, even when I'm not pumped up with baby-making hormones. I've been…prickly.''

No kidding.

''I'll try and remember that.'' He kept his tone calm, the way he would around a spooked mare. ''When you didn't return to the table, I feared the stalker might have…''

Rhianna turned to him and really looked into his eyes. She must have seen his worry because her voice softened. ''I really *am* sorry.'' Her hand fluttered at her side. ''I didn't mean to cause—''

''I know.''

He took her hand. Although he sensed she wanted to yank it away, she didn't. Probably because she felt badly for snapping at him. Rafe didn't care. He'd take any excuse to touch her, to show her he did care about her health and safety.

They strolled through the alley toward the street and his car. ''Your truck repairs won't be completed until tomorrow.''

''Just when did you arrange this?''

''While you were in the rest room. And I reserved a hotel room for tonight—two hotel rooms.''

''Whoa!'' She jerked her hand from his, mistrust in her eyes, and scowled at him. ''I can't afford repairs. I'm going back to my house and my parents. I'm not spending the night with you—two rooms or not. I'm sure they connect.''

Still unsettled by her disappearance in the restaurant, thoroughly annoyed that she'd pulled her hand from his at the first excuse, he wondered why he was so hot and bothered over this woman. Was it just because she carried his child? He'd like to think so, but Rhianna always had a way of putting the spurs to his temper. Still, he tried to be patient, ignored her crack about the hotel room and reined in his anger. "I'll pay for the truck repairs."

She tucked a flyaway strand of hair behind her ear. "You will not. Our horses may have had extra medical expenses these past few months, but we pay our own bills."

He folded his arms across his chest and refused to let her ramrod the issue. "I don't want my baby riding in an unsafe vehicle."

She planted her fists on her hips and glared at him with defiance. "McClouds don't take charity."

"And I'm not offering it. I owe you. Owe you for medical bills. Owe you for baby stuff. Owe you for time you lost from work." She opened her mouth to protest, but he wouldn't let her get a word in until he finished. Just because she was pregnant didn't mean she could have everything her way. "As for returning to your folks' house, I don't want you going anywhere the stalker can find you. And the baby. I'll only be with you if you need me." And from the look on her face, hell would ice over before that happened.

Rhianna opened her fingers, then closed them back into fists, then opened them again with a shake. "I can't stay—not even if I wanted to. Dad needs help with the foal."

"He'll manage without you."

"I have animal husbandry classes at school. I've been attending part time for years and I almost have my degree."

"You can make up the classes."

"I need clothes."

"We'll buy some."

"Who gave you permission to take over my life?"

He didn't bother answering such a ludicrous accusation. Instead he spoke more quickly than his normal muted drawl. "And don't even start harping about money again. It's insulting to think that I wouldn't support my—our—child."

Rhianna chuckled, a lightning mood switch he much preferred to her anger. "Did anyone ever tell you that you're stubborn?"

"*Moi?* I'm the easygoing Sutton. My brother Cam is the hardheaded one."

She shook her head and grinned as he opened the passenger door of his car for her. "You're easygoing as long as you get your way."

He nodded, much preferring her smiles to her scowls, even if the smiles did make him ache. "Now you have me all figured out."

Before Rafe could close the door, an ice cream vendor on a bicycle pulling a three-wheeled freezer approached, jingling his bells. Rhianna started to lick her lips, and Rafe grinned at her insatiable appetite.

He reached for his wallet. "Chocolate, strawberry or vanilla?"

"Neapolitan, please."

He should have known she'd crave all three flavors. He purchased the treat, and as she ate, he drove through the Mile High City, concentrating on traffic and his route. He came to the city fairly often and knew his way around Denver's excellent museums, the historic homes in residential neighborhoods and several lovely old bed-and-breakfast inns that brimmed with the city's colorful past.

When Rhianna had finished eating her ice cream and neatly folded the wrapper into a tiny square, she leaned back in her seat. He thought she simply needed to rest her neck, but as he passed Congress Park on Eighth Avenue, he noticed her scanning the rearview mirror every thirty seconds or so.

"Anything wrong?"

"Just habit."

"Rhianna, do you have any idea who might be after you? Or why?"

"Not a clue. That's what's so frustrating." She exhaled a sigh of frustration. "Even the police said the stalker's actions don't make much sense. The stalker never comes close enough to talk to me, but threatens, always from a distance. What's the point in scaring me?"

RAFE AND RHIANNA CHECKED into the hotel after he'd convinced her that the stalker would never find her here and that returning home was unsafe. Rafe walked her over the marble floors and past the cigar room with its leather chairs and rich men's atmosphere. And damn him, he'd reserved a suite that included two bedrooms, a living area decorated in a Southwestern style of soft russets and eggshell blues, and a full-size kitchen. White roses filled a crystal vase on the fireplace mantel and their scent mixed with jars of potpourri. Today's *Denver Times* lay neatly folded next to a fruit basket.

Rhianna ignored the newspaper and picked up a green apple. She polished it on her sleeve, then bit into it with a satisfying crunch. She'd already phoned her father, who'd told her that a rest would do her good. She'd thought he'd sounded much too satisfied with himself after she'd admitted she was staying with Rafe.

But Rhianna had no time to dwell on Daniel's smug tone. Rafe Sutton, the tall man in front of her, was causing too many conflicting emotions. She only wanted him there if he wanted to be. Duty wasn't a good enough reason. Neither was guilt. She appraised him from head to boots, taking in the stubborn angle of his masculine chin, the smoldering gray eyes, the lips that she remembered when she closed her eyes at night, the broad chest that had pillowed her head more softly than any down pillow, the slim hips that gyrated with just the right amount of... *Don't go there.*

He doesn't want you, she reminded herself. He'd only come back because Daniel had called him. And now Rafe felt obligated to help her. Why couldn't he have left her alone?

He probably had no idea how painful she found it to be near him. And she would never, ever let him know.

Eight and a half months ago, she'd given Rafe a part of herself she'd never surrendered before and probably never would again. She'd taken a chance in going to bed with him, but she'd wanted him for so long, she couldn't have denied her desire. And that night he'd lived up to her expectations. After their lovemaking, she'd hoped he would come back to her, maybe explore something more permanent, but when he hadn't, she'd done her best to put him out of her mind. She'd known he wasn't the marrying kind. Even after she discovered her pregnancy, she'd never considered using her condition to lasso him in.

She'd thought the acutely painful memories would fade. They hadn't. But being close to him, smelling his scent, looking into his eyes and knowing he didn't care for her the way she'd dreamed, made her angry and sad and thoroughly confused that she could still respond to a man who clearly didn't want her.

She was annoyed with herself, angry at him. How could he be so stupid to throw away what they could have had? She didn't need constant reminders of what might have been. She didn't need him.

She nibbled her apple and debated throwing him out of his own hotel suite. But that would be callous, rude.

Yet what right did he have to just show up and take over her problems?

Rafe gestured for her to sit, and took up a pad and pen. "We need a plan."

"Why?"

"So when we divert from it, we know what we're diverting from." When she frowned in puzzlement, he ran his fingers through that lovely dark hair of his. "That was a joke to relax you."

"Oh. Good thing you don't make your living as a comedian."

"Very funny." He pushed the notepad and pen toward her, and she recalled those same hands so intimately caressing her flesh, setting her on fire with pleasure. "Why don't you start by making a list."

"Of?" Unwilling to put down her apple for fear he'd notice her shaking fingers, she transferred the fruit from her right hand to her left, then picked up the pen.

"Everyone you've dated for the last five years. Everyone who's angry at you. Anyone your father's fired. Angry relatives, that kind of thing."

She dropped the pen. She didn't want to tell him how few men she'd dated. Didn't want him prying into every corner of her life. "I already went through this with the police."

Rafe's gray eyes glinted with steel and the tiny flecks of black in his irises glittered. "Then it should be easier this time."

She could see he had no intention of giving in. No intention of stopping this inquisition until he had what he wanted. He'd been the same way the night of their child's conception. Thorough. Uncompromising. Commanding.

Ignoring her obvious reluctance, he picked up the pen. "I'll do the writing. Just give me names." He started scribbling. "We can put Duncan Phillips at the top of the list."

"Duncan?"

"Has he forgiven you for turning down his proposal?"

"No, but—"

"Has he forgiven you for stabling your mare near his stallion?"

"No, but—"

"And he lives in Denver. He has the means, opportunity and a motive to harass you."

"Duncan isn't crazy. He's merely…eccentric."

"Uh-huh."

She had the feeling Rafe was patronizing her again.

But maybe his thoughts on the matter were clearer. Rafe didn't have the disadvantage of knowing Duncan Phillips. Rafe's thoughts weren't colored by her memories of a Duncan who adored his horses and a man who'd treated her with the utmost courtesy and respect—until she'd rejected him. Duncan's temper had let loose then and he'd turned nasty. But the man wasn't violent, was he?

"Who else?" Rafe prodded. "I need your help, Rhianna. I can't do this by myself."

His speech might be gentle, but she still didn't want him to delve into her life. She remained silent.

"Your father's worked on half the ranches around Denver. Any of the hands ever make a pass at you?"

"Most of them." She grimaced and answered despite her intention not to. "I hardly think that qualifies them to be put on your list."

"*Our* list. And I can't blame a man for…"

She cocked her brow and watched his eyes. "Going after what you wanted?"

Eyes gentle and rueful, he gazed at her seemingly without guilt. "You're a beautiful woman."

"That's why you wrote me so many touching love letters."

He winced and his quicksilver eyes darkened with shadows. "You can't get past that, can you?"

"Nope." Finished with the apple, she tossed the core into the trash and folded her arms across her chest, portraying strength in order to hide the cutting sorrow she couldn't put aside. "You want me to spill my life to you. Well, it may not be very exciting, but it's *my* life. And it's private."

"Is your privacy more important to you than your safety?"

She remained silent.

"What about the baby's safety?" he pressed.

His logic fired up her temper. "Damn you. Just because we put a name from my past on a list doesn't mean the baby and I will be safe."

He threw down the pen, straddled the seat and leaned back until he balanced on the chair's back legs, studying her with an intensity that made her want to squirm. "So what do you want from me?"

"Nothing."

"Because I've stayed away for the last eight and a half months?"

"Now you're catching on."

"Look, you knew from the start that one night was all we might have."

"I knew that then. I know it better now."

"But now we have a baby to consider. If we can't figure out who's stalking you, there's only one way to keep you and the baby safe."

"I'm listening."

"You can come live with me."

What? Live in his house, see him every day—so that when she finally left, she could spend the rest of her days grieving over what she couldn't have? "Excuse me? I thought you said I should come live with you."

"It's a good idea. Our ranch is isolated. We can have the hands guard the road in, keep an eye out for strangers. You'd be safe there."

"No."

"No?" He laced his hands behind his head and

tilted back even farther, until she was sure he would
topple over. But he didn't. Instead he looked incred-
ibly sexy, and that annoyed her all the more.

Still she made an effort to keep her tone reasonable.
"I don't owe you reasons for the choices I make,
Rafe. I don't owe you anything."

"You've chosen to bear our child. Don't you owe
the baby a safe place to grow up?"

Rhianna had no answer for that particular question.
But no matter her circumstances, she'd never regret
her decision to have this baby. Somehow she would
find a way to keep it safe. Already she loved her child,
knew she'd do whatever she could to protect it.

"Okay. I'll stay at the ranch until the baby's born."

She would accompany Rafe to the Sutton ranch,
since she agreed her baby would be safe there. She
would give up the luxury of having her own doctor
there when she gave birth. Give up her mother, who'd
agreed to coach her on her breathing. Give up the
security of her father's arms afterward. Although going with Rafe would deprive her of sharing the most
important moment of her life with people who loved
her, she had to put the baby's safety first.

Just thinking through the possibilities tired Rhianna. She let out a huge yawn, and Rafe instantly
rocked to his feet. "You look as if you need a nap.
Why don't you lie down for a little while and rest?"

She should argue with him for fussing over her, but
fatigue struck like a charging bull. As she waddled
into her room and collapsed on the bed, Rafe drew
the shades and blinds, then spread a blanket over her.

She sensed a tension in him, but his voice remained

tender. "Sleep tight and don't worry. We'll think of something."

RAFE CALLED HIS DAD. Sometimes having a Colorado state senator in the family was handy. After Rafe explained the problems, the senator called a friend at the university, and Rhianna got an automatic extension to finish her classes. Rafe received the name of a first-class detective agency and phoned there next. The Sutton name produced immediate attention.

Next Rafe phoned a maternity shop and had clothes for Rhianna sent to the hotel, since he had no intention of letting her go back home. He wouldn't expose her to more danger. Then Rafe arranged for a Sutton stable boy to help Daniel in Rhianna's place. Finally he called her mother and asked Rhea McCloud if she could join them in Highview, the town nearest the Sutton ranch, when Rhianna's time drew near. When the sweet woman assured him she and her husband would be happy to make the drive, Rafe felt a measure of relief.

Last, he put in a call to his brother, Dr. Cameron Sutton. "Cam, what kind of obstetric facilities does Highview Hospital have?"

"Is she high risk?"

"I didn't ask. She eats a lot."

"That's helpful. Stress can bring on the contractions, so you should keep her calm."

"Don't you remember Rhianna's temper?"

"I was in medical school when Daniel worked for us. But I think I recall a teenager with cinnamon hair following you around like she thought you hung the moon."

Rafe's gut clenched as he realized how well Cam had pegged the girl and the woman. "That's Rhianna, and she's never really calm...."

"Don't worry. Even if the baby comes a little early, it's old enough that there shouldn't be any complications."

"I think I can—"

"Sounds to me like you weren't thinking much at all."

He could almost see Cam's smug grin. Rafe tried to set him straight. "Hey, protection fails sometimes."

"You should marry her."

"I'm not—"

"Babies need mothers and fathers."

"Mothers and father should be compatible."

"Why?" Cam asked. Rafe was sure his brother was just trying to needle him. But Cam continued, "Compatible might be boring. Maybe you need a little spice in your life. I'm thinking hot cinnamon—"

"Look, I called for your medical opinion. If she comes to the ranch and goes into labor, will we have enough time to get her to the hospital?"

"First babies are notoriously slow to arrive. But if the contractions do come hard and quick, you could fly her in the chopper."

"Thanks, Cam." A knock on the door to the suite cut the conversation short.

Rafe opened the door. A middle-aged, squat man with curly, blond hair held up a picture ID. "Joe Brown from the Lyle Detective Agency. I understand you have some kind of emergency, sir?"

Rafe let the detective inside, hoping that Rhianna's

nap would continue until they finished. By now he realized that she wouldn't appreciate the detective checking out her friends, family and acquaintances. Yet Rafe had to place her safety over her wishes.

He quickly explained Rhianna's problem to Joe Brown, immediately believing in the man's honesty and integrity, since the senator had recommended him.

"And what exactly do you want our agency to do?" Joe asked. "You can hire a team to protect Ms. McCloud round the clock, but to be effective, we'd need Ms. McCloud's full cooperation. From what you've indicated, she seems reluctant to have her privacy compromised. And to tell you the truth, most clients detest close surveillance." He paused, then suggested, "I can also do background checks and see if we find anything suspicious."

"Background checks on whom?" Rhianna padded on bare feet into the room. The circles under her eyes were just as dark as before her nap, and Rafe suspected she hadn't slept. But she had enough energy for her eyes to flash with annoyance.

"Rhianna, I'd like you to meet Joe Brown from the Lyle Detective Agency," Rafe said smoothly, hoping she wouldn't cause a fuss. Cam had said to keep her calm, but that seemed nigh onto impossible with the way she was scowling at him.

"You've hired him without even talking to me?" Rhianna's tone rose in displeasure.

"I didn't want to wake you." Rafe thought his voice remained smooth, but could tell from her expression that she considered his excuse lame. "We were just talking over our options when you came in."

"I see."

"I'm not sure you do, Ms. McCloud," Joe said. "There are some sick, really sick, folks out there. Someone is watching you. Taunting you. I believe it's only a matter of time before he makes a move."

"Thanks, I feel so much safer now."

Rhianna's words might be sarcastic, but Rafe had seen the flicker of fear in her eyes before she straightened her spine, jutted out her chin and hid the emotion. At her show of stubborn courage, his heart went out to her. Rafe wanted to ease her worry, but she kept refusing his help.

Joe turned to Rafe. "If she won't—"

"Please don't talk about me as if I'm not here," Rhianna interrupted softly. "Despite my irritation with Rafe for making decisions without at least consulting me, I won't let my feelings interfere with the baby's safety."

Rafe should have known she would be sensible. She might not accept his help for herself. She might not want him around. She might not want a detective snooping into her life, but Rhianna would make the right choice for the baby's sake.

"Good." Joe opened his briefcase and handed Rafe a contract. "I'd recommend we start with the background search of friends, co-workers, business associates and relatives." Joe fixed Rhianna with a pointed stare. "As long as Rafe stays with you, I believe we can hold off on round-the-clock protection."

Rafe looked at Rhianna. "What do you think?"

Before she could answer, someone else knocked on

the door. Rhianna's brow rose in question. Rafe stood and tried to look casual as he wondered if her temper would flare again. "I took the liberty of buying you some clothes, since you won't be going home for a while."

Rafe opened the door, and the bellboy placed several large shopping bags in the foyer. Rafe tipped him, and the kid pulled a white velvet jewelry box from his pocket. "Oh, I almost forgot, sir. This was messengered over. It's for Rhianna McCloud."

Rafe frowned. "I...I—"

Rhianna walked up behind him. "I won't marry you, Rafe. Send it back."

He couldn't blame Rhianna for her assumption that he'd bought her a ring. The gold-embossed Biddle and Baines logo on the box belonged to a well-known Denver jeweler, their distinctive white box with gold lettering familiar to Denver's wealthier citizens. But Rafe didn't like engagement rings, didn't like the kind of commitment the jewelry represented. "I didn't order any ring."

"You didn't?" Rhianna looked from the jewelry box in the bellboy's hand to Rafe. A blush started up her neck and flushed her cheeks as she realized her mistake. "When Duncan proposed, his ring came in a box from Biddle and Baines."

"Let me see it, please." Joe took the box from the bellhop, fingertips holding the edges. He held it to his ear, then shook the box. "It's not ticking."

Rhianna leaned around Rafe to see. Rafe held her back, a suspicious tingle tightening the back of his neck, telling him that something was wrong.

Joe set the Biddle and Baines box on the dining table and carefully pried it open.

Chapter Four

Foul-smelling ashes overflowed the jewelry box and smeared the dining room table.

The stalker had found her.

After all the precautions Rafe had taken to hide her away from her friends and co-workers, the stalker had found her, probably another tail they hadn't seen. The message seemed clear. She couldn't run far enough. She couldn't hide.

As the ugly black ashes fell out of the pristine white velvet box embossed with gold lettering, Rhianna shuddered. Rafe put his arm around her shoulders, but not even the heat of his flesh could warm her as an icy chill settled in her gut.

For once she welcomed the comfort Rafe's solid presence could give her. She no longer wanted to go through this alone. And who better to protect her than the man who had put the baby inside her? He had a very good reason to ensure her safety. His child's life was at stake.

Joe poked through the ashes with the tip of his pen. "Nothing dangerous. Just ashes."

"What's the point of sending something like

that?'' Rhianna asked, hoping the men hadn't come to the same conclusion she had. The stalker was toying with her. Well, she wasn't anyone's damned toy, and as anger flooded through her, it banished her fears to the back of her mind, so she could hold her head up and go on.

''He wants to scare you,'' Rafe muttered.

''But why?'' Rhianna asked.

He gathered her into his arms. ''Maybe he's sick. He wants to show you that he knows exactly where you are.''

Joe grimaced. ''I doubt I can retrieve fingerprints off the velvet but I'll try.'' He paused, then continued, ''I'll bet the messenger who gave the bellhop this box is long gone. The messenger may not even work for a real service. However, the Biddle and Baines box might give us some clues.''

Rafe looked into Rhianna's face. She nodded that she was okay now. He left her side to pull out a phone book, then looked up a number and dialed. ''This is Senator Sutton's son. No, not Dr. Cameron. Nope, this isn't Chase Sutton, either. I'm Rafe. I'd like an appointment with the manager, please.''

Rhianna had always known the power of the Sutton name, but she'd never had it used for her benefit. When she thought of people using their names to obtain special treatment, she normally considered it pretentious. But right now she was grateful. Any help in ending this ordeal was appreciated.

The jewelry store wasn't far from the hotel. Within a half hour, the pleasant-faced owner-manager, Saul Biddle escorted Rhianna, Rafe and Joe into his inner sanctum.

Plush carpets muffled their steps. Mahogany paneling, an antique desk and a sideboard full of crystal liqueur decanters gave the dimly lit room an old-world ambiance. A secretary wearing a severe black suit served coffee and cinnamon crumb cakes.

Rhianna skipped the coffee but helped herself to two of the cakes while she surveyed the owner-manager. She supposed his indistinguishable features and unremarkable eyes made him a perfect foil for the magnificent jewels she'd seen as she'd walked through the exclusive store.

Saul waited through introductions and until everyone was settled comfortably before asking, "What can I do for you?"

Rhianna expected Joe to take charge, but Rafe spoke first, his Western drawl slow and polite. "We're hoping you can help us find the person who is stalking Ms. McCloud."

Saul sipped his coffee. "That's a little out of my field."

Joe placed the velvet jewelry box on Saul's desk. "Maybe not."

"Someone sent that to me," Rhianna said softly. "Inside are ashes."

"Ashes?" Saul frowned. "The stalker used *our* jewelry box to deliver some kind of threat?"

Rhianna realized her problem might be outside Saul Biddle's area of expertise, but he caught on quickly. "An ex-boyfriend of mine, Duncan Phillips, bought me an engagement ring from this store."

"Did he ever return the ring?" Rafe asked.

"What would that prove?" Saul asked. "He could have returned the ring without the box."

"It's a place to start," Rafe said. "Especially if he kept the ring."

Saul looked from Rafe to Rhianna. "We don't normally open our records to the public, but under the circumstances, I'll try to help."

Rhianna wondered if the manager would have been so helpful if she'd come in alone and asked for help, wondered if she'd have gotten past the secretary who guarded the office door. Once again she was grateful for Rafe's help.

Saul pressed a button on his desk. A moment later his secretary walked in. "Sylvia, could you please bring me Duncan Phillips's file? And I'd like a printout of every customer who purchased a ring in the last two years."

"Thank you," Rafe said softly. "We do appreciate your help."

Joe leaned forward. "May I ask why you only want the records for the past two years?"

"We switched designs then." Saul pointed to the box. "The hinge on this box is hidden. On our old ones, the hinge showed."

"That's a bit of luck," Joe murmured.

Rhianna didn't feel lucky. The cinnamon cake sat like a lump of clay in her stomach. And the baby had chosen this moment to start practicing soccer kicks. Rafe must have noticed her twinge of discomfort because he started rubbing the back of her neck. "We're going to figure this out. You'll see."

His soft words should have annoyed her. She didn't need to be reassured like a child. And yet she'd carried the burden alone for so long, it was easy to let Rafe take on some of the load. Briefly she reminded herself not to get used to Rafe's being there for her. He would stay until the baby's birth or the crisis passed—whichever came first—and then he'd be gone from her life again.

"Could an employee have stolen a box?" Rafe asked.

Saul shook his head. "We'd have noticed. We keep a careful inventory."

The secretary returned with a file and a computerized printout. Rafe handed the long list to Rhianna. "See if you recognize any names."

As she perused the list, Rhianna refrained from whistling aloud. It included not only names, but items bought and the purchase price. She couldn't believe how many people could afford a luxury purchase that cost more than the McClouds' mortgage on their home. Chase and Cameron Sutton had both bought their wives rings in this store. No wonder Saul Biddle had opened his books to Rafe.

Rhianna often forgot the wealth of the Suttons. All the brothers seemed down-to-earth, concerned about their land, their cows and each other, making her forget their affluence.

"Duncan Phillips didn't return the ring he purchased," Saul told them.

Rhianna let out a soft gasp of surprise.

"What?" Rafe squeezed her hand reassuringly, but this time his attempt didn't make her feel any better.

For a moment the names blurred in front of her. Then she pulled herself together. "Janet Stone bought a ring here. So did Judge Stuart. While Joe continues his investigation and before we go into hiding, I think we should pay a visit to some of the people on this list.''

RAFE HAD KNOWN Duncan Phillips for years but had never visited the man's Denver estate. He'd heard Duncan had made his fortune when his technical company had gone public and the stock had soared. Duncan had since retired from the high-tech world to become a horse breeder. He had a reputation with the ladies and a reputation for gambling huge amounts of money at the track.

Still the opulence of Duncan's estate took Rafe by surprise. The Suttons' wealth was in cattle and land, acres and acres of land that took a man two days to ride across. But Duncan's home looked like a European castle with fancy turrets, stone walls and frilly Victorian ironwork. The lush grounds were immaculate, and they passed through a guarded gate with security cameras. So much for taking Duncan by surprise.

A maid opened the front door and led them to a study. Duncan Phillips, dressed in immaculately pressed jodhpurs and shiny riding boots, and holding a crop, opened the massive front door and greeted Rhianna with a superior smirk at her extended belly. "Come in. Come in. Can I offer you a drink?"

Rafe shook the man's hand, realizing that Duncan might have the cash flow to support his hobbies, but he wasn't any gentleman. The man seemed to take immense pleasure in taking Rhianna's left hand and placing a kiss there while he stared at her ringless finger, deliberately calling attention to her unmarried and pregnant state.

Rhianna's only reaction was to lift her chin higher. "Sorry to drop in so unexpectedly, Duncan."

Duncan smirked again. "Well, at least this time I don't believe you rode over on a mare in heat. So to what do I owe the pleasure?"

He'd mounted the walls of the study with hunting trophies: heads of elk, tiger, boar, even a rhino that she suspected was an endangered species. Rhianna shuddered slightly and avoided glancing at the dead animals.

Despite her condition, she seemed to be holding up well to the stress of the latest "gift" from the stalker. Despite Duncan's not-so-subtle attempts to put her in her place, Rhianna looked ready to confront her former boyfriend. Her green eyes looked as calm as a still pool, her face fresh as spring air.

Upon seeing Duncan and Rhianna together again, Rafe knew at once that Duncan was not the man for Rhianna. She was sunlight and warmth to his high-tech ice. Duncan's house wasn't a home but a statement to the world that the man inside had arrived. The idea of a child playing in this office with its expensive knickknacks within easy reach and dead animals staring down with glassy-eyed sorrow was ludicrous.

Rhianna would have regretted it if she'd accepted Duncan's proposal. But had Duncan seen the breakup the same way? Obviously the man was accustomed to winning. Rafe suspected her refusal had hurt Duncan's pride much more than his heart—but enough to stalk her?

Rhianna sat on the edge of a chair as if she didn't

want to become too comfortable. "I need to ask you about the ring you bought for me."

Duncan reached into his cigar box and frowned. "I don't see how that's your concern now."

"Would you please not light that cigar?" she requested politely, refusing to be drawn into Duncan's game of petty innuendos.

"You never minded before."

Rafe remained silent, letting Rhianna speak. He'd always admired a woman who stood up for herself, and hoped Rhianna would pass that magnificent trait on to their child.

"The smoke's not good for the baby," Rhianna explained, her tone calm. But Rafe could see a flash of temper in her eyes.

Duncan reached for his lighter, obviously not caring about the baby's health. "It's my office."

"Fine. Just don't complain if I vomit all over your Oriental rug, okay?"

In response, Duncan tossed the lighter onto the desk and clamped his still unlit cigar between his teeth. Rafe bit his tongue to keep from laughing outright. Rhianna was clearly way too much woman for Duncan Phillips.

"Duncan, could I look at the ring you bought for me?" Rhianna asked, her voice sweet as summer.

Rafe realized how smart she was by not admitting that they already knew Duncan hadn't returned the ring. He settled back in his chair, watching Duncan carefully, still content to let Rhianna ask the questions.

Duncan maintained a poker face. His eyes gave away nothing. "Why do you want to see the ring?"

"Someone sent me a jewelry box from Biddle and Baines—only instead of a ring, the box held ashes."

Duncan glared at her. "You think I sent you a box with ashes in it?"

"Of course not. I just want to discount you as a suspect—" she waved her hand as if shooing away an insignificant fly "—for the police report I have to fill out."

"Police report?"

"Senator Sutton has taken an interest," Rhianna stated, "and insists we fill out the paperwork correctly, just in case reporters sniff out the story."

Duncan's eyes widened with horror. "The senator? Reporters? I don't want my name attached to your sordid—"

"Fine. Can I see the ring?"

Duncan tapped his cigar on his desk. "When you refused my proposal, I returned the ring."

Rafe thought it time to remind Duncan that Rhianna wasn't alone in the room. "Don't lie to her. We know you didn't return it."

Duncan didn't appear particularly upset that they'd caught him in an outright lie. Instead, he looked longingly at the lighter, then decisively placed the cigar back in the box, rose and poured himself a drink. "I was hoping Rhianna would change her mind and agree to be my wife."

"So you *do* still have the ring," Rhianna said excitedly. "Where is it?"

Duncan shook his head. "I'm afraid not. When you refused my offer, I was upset. I crushed the box and threw it away."

"You threw away that expensive—"

"Oh, I still have the ring. I just tossed the box."

Crushed it and threw it away. The man sounded sincere, but a minute ago he'd lied to them. He might have just been embarrassed to admit that he'd hoped she'd change her mind about his marriage proposal. Returning the ring was the equivalent of ending his hopes. Rafe could understand how he'd hang on to it, how he wouldn't want to admit to failure. But now Duncan offered such a flimsy excuse for throwing away the box that Rafe had to consider him their number one suspect.

"Did anyone see you crush the box?" Rhianna asked. "Maybe a maid?"

Duncan shook his head. "I still don't understand what all the fuss is about. So what if someone sent you a box of ashes? Why are the police and the senator interested?"

"Someone is stalking Rhianna. And when we prove who that person is, he'll go to jail."

"If anyone should go to jail, it's her." Duncan slapped his drink on the desk, and the liquor sloshed over the side. "She's the one who stole my prize stallion's sperm."

Rhianna pushed herself to her feet. She didn't say a word to refute Duncan's accusation, didn't dignify his statement with a reply. "It's time to leave."

RHIANNA YAWNED AS SHE and Rafe drove to Judge Stuart's courtroom. She couldn't decide whether Duncan was lying about the jewelry box or not. It still seemed odd to her that three people at her father's party had bought rings from Biddle and Baines. But the horse set was rich, and the store famous for its innovative designs.

Rhianna realized rich people tended to shop in the same stores. But that didn't mean the wealthy were alike in character or temperament.

When she'd seen Rafe Sutton and Duncan Phillips together today, she'd known she'd made the correct decision to reject Duncan's proposal. Duncan just didn't stir her blood. With Rafe, she noticed the lift of his brow, the tilt of his head, sensed his moods without effort. He merely needed to share the same air she breathed, and her senses instantly focused on him.

And that made accepting his help all the harder. Every time Rafe showed her consideration, every time they shared a look, a thought, a car ride, she had to remind herself he didn't want her.

Rafe was here for one reason. To protect the child they'd created together. And every time she remembered, she became angry with him all over again.

She didn't want his friendly hand massaging her neck. She didn't want him to buy her clothes. She didn't want to go live in his house, on his ranch, on Sutton land. But how could she live with him and silence her feelings?

She couldn't disassociate herself from her feelings that easily, and wanted to protect herself from the pain of another rejection. She refused to even consider that this time Rafe might realize what he hadn't before—that they were good together. She wouldn't make the mistake of building up her hopes again only to have them dashed in disappointment.

Rafe was Rafe. Either he wouldn't change or he couldn't.

Just thinking about her predicament made Rhianna tired and thoroughly overstressed. She napped, and opened her eyes again just as Rafe parked in front of the courthouse. Within minutes they'd passed the metal detectors and security guard.

Judge Stuart's secretary ushered them straight into his chambers. His distinguished suit helped counter the effect of thinning hair slicked in a comb-over to hide his balding head. At their entrance, the judge removed his feet from his desk, but Rhianna caught a glimpse of a gun strapped to his ankle.

"Death threats," the judge explained to Rhianna as he shook Rafe's hand. "Every case has a winner and a loser. The losers often threaten to come back and… Where are my manners? Please have a seat. Can I get you anything? A cola? Water?"

Rhianna settled into an overstuffed leather chair. "Thanks, I'm fine."

The judge looked from Rafe to Rhianna with a warm smile. "You've come to ask me to perform another Sutton wedding?"

Rhianna had heard that the judge had married one of Rafe's brothers. The judge and the senator went way back—and the judge obviously felt familiar enough with Rafe to place him on the spot. Rhianna turned to Rafe, wondering if he would squirm at the question. She should have known better.

Rafe shook his head. "I'm afraid another happy occasion will have to wait. Rhianna's being stalked."

"If one of my ex-cons is violating parole, I'll be happy to lock him up."

Rhianna couldn't blame the judge for leaping to such a conclusion. She supposed he'd placed many people behind bars. Still, he seemed so gleeful about his job.

"Actually, we don't know the stalker's identity," Rafe explained.

The judge turned up his palms. "Then how can I help?"

Rhianna leaned forward and tried to read the man's eyes. "We need to ask you about a ring you bought at Biddle and Baines, your honor."

She saw nothing but confusion on his face. "What does an anniversary present for my wife have to do with your problem?"

"The stalker sent Rhianna a ring box filled with ashes. The manager at Biddle and Baines was kind enough to show us a customer list, and we're speaking to everyone on that list Rhianna knows."

The judge nodded. "That makes sense."

"Would your wife still have the ring box?" Rafe asked with just the right amount of respect and concern.

Judge Stuart shrugged. "You can ask her if you like—she's not talking to me. We divorced last year." He smiled bitterly. "She kept the house, the ring and the stock portfolio."

"I'm sorry," Rhianna said softly.

The judge locked eyes with Rafe. "When Karen picked me over your father, I thought our marriage would last forever."

Rafe scratched his chin and looked puzzled. "I don't understand."

"Back in the good old days, Highview had two

rival high school football teams. Your dad played quarterback and defeated us for the chance to go to the state championship. That set the pattern, I suppose,'' the judge said philosophically. ''I ran and lost against your father for sheriff and mayor, then for a senate seat. But I always figured I was the lucky man. I had Karen.'' He wrote an address on a piece of paper. ''Excuse me. No need for you to listen to an old man go on and on about the past. I'm not usually so maudlin. Here's Karen's new address and phone number. She's remarried, to a plastic surgeon.''

Ms. KAREN PRESCOTT answered her phone and invited them to come by after dinner. Rhianna had wished Rafe could just ask her about the box over the phone. All this driving around and talking took a toll on her energy level. Yet she knew she needed to see that jewelry box with her own eyes.

Rafe parked in the four-car driveway between a Rolls Royce and a Viper. Ms. Prescott answered the door, but if she hadn't introduced herself, Rhianna wouldn't have believed she'd been married to the judge for thirty years. She didn't look a day over twenty-nine. Her platinum hair glistened, a soft halo of light. Her creamy skin didn't have a wrinkle...or a laugh line.

Next to the glamorous Ms. Prescott, Rhianna felt as fat as a house. The woman thrust a white velvet box into Rafe's hand before he had a chance to say hello. ''This what you wanted to see? I'm sorry to hurry you, but we're on the way to a charity event where my husband is the guest of honor.''

''This is the box that came with the anniversary

ring your ex-husband purchased for you?'' Rafe asked.

"The judge had many faults, but, stinginess wasn't one of them. He also bought me a bracelet and earrings to match the ring. Of course, they came in different shaped boxes.''

"Thank you so much, Ms. Prescott. We won't take any more of your time.''

The woman took back the box from Rafe, and Rhianna noticed the aquamarine on her pinky finger, the twenty-plus-carat sapphire ring beside it. She looked from the ring to the woman. "Please, just a few more minutes of your time. Did the judge buy you any other rings during the last two years?''

Karen Prescott almost frowned, then seemed to recall that any expression would mar the perfect symmetry of her face. "He bought me jewelry for my birthday, for my anniversary and for Christmas. What of it?''

"Did all the rings come in white velvet boxes?'' Rhianna persisted, even though hunger pangs told her that she needed to eat soon.

"Of course.''

"Do you still have *all* of them?''

"In the vault.'' The woman started to close the door, seeming nervous about staying in sight. Was she afraid of her ex-husband? Rhianna wondered. Or was she herself just imagining things?

"You're sure?''

"Very. I had to open them all to find this ring. Each is in its box—I'm very meticulous about my jewelry.''

"Thank you, Ms. Prescott.'' Rhianna fought to

keep disappointment from her tone. "You've been very—"

"I'm so sorry. But you really must go." The woman firmly closed the door behind them.

Rhianna had to admit the judge had been a long shot. She didn't know the man well. What reason would he have had to stalk her, anyway? she wondered as they drove away. At least they could cross him off their very short list.

She turned to Rafe. "Looks like we came up empty again."

"Hal and Janet Stone live in Highview. We can talk to them tomorrow."

"I barely know the Stones. And what motive would they have to stalk me?" Just thinking about the possibilities tired Rhianna out. The box could have been stolen or taken out of someone's garbage. There were too many possibilities to pin all their hopes on one alone. But the empty box was their only lead, so it made sense to at least follow through. If Rafe persisted in his idea of taking her to his ranch, she didn't know how she'd find the energy to fight him. "Maybe that detective has found something."

"It's unlikely the Stones are the culprits, but I'd like to narrow down every possibility." He glanced at her with compassion, as if he could read her weariness. "We'll phone Joe after dinner. Right now you look as if you need some food."

Food! Rhianna smiled. "You know just how to make me perk up." At least they could relax and mull over her situation. Headlights in the rearview mirror caught Rhianna's eye and she grabbed Rafe's hand.

"Rafe, that car has been following us since we left Ms. Prescott's house."

Rafe looked in the rearview mirror. "Which car?"

"The silver sedan with the tinted windows."

"I see it." Rafe made a quick but controlled U-turn. "Hang on. Let's go talk to the driver."

Chapter Five

Rhianna put her hand over her stomach. "Maybe a confrontation isn't a good idea."

At least Rafe didn't speed. He drove carefully, competently, without any visible tension in his grip of the steering wheel.

Still, fear galloped through Rhianna like a runaway horse. Rafe easily pulled alongside the silver sedan, which had stopped in a restaurant parking lot.

Rafe parked behind the sedan, unfastened his seat belt and opened his door. "Stay here."

Rhianna didn't say a word in argument. But no way would she allow Rafe to face her stalker alone. Unarmed.

Reaching into her pocket, she took comfort in the cold steel of her gun. As Rafe approached the sedan, she flicked off the safety, then opened her car door slowly, careful not to make a sound. She didn't want Rafe to hear her or see her as she waddled behind him and aimed the gun at the driver's window.

Rafe must have sensed her. "Don't you ever think of the baby first?"

Rhianna hefted the gun. ''The baby needs a father just as much as a mother.''

Rafe's whisper rose in aggravation. ''I'd like the baby to make it into this world in one piece.''

''I'm careful.''

In the deepening darkness of dusk, Rhianna couldn't see through the tinted glass. A whirring sound made her fingers tighten around the gun's grip, but the noise was only the car's window rolling down.

Joe, the detective Rafe had hired, nodded a sheepish hello. ''Spotted me tailing you, did you?''

''You!'' Rhianna flicked the gun's safety back on and started to return her weapon to her pocket.

But Rafe took the gun from her with a long look of resignation, then checked the safety catch before returning the weapon to her, handle first. ''You never did listen worth a damn.''

Rhianna tossed her hair over her shoulder. ''I only listen to smart advice. Walking up to a possible stalker isn't the brightest move you've ever made.''

With a careless shrug, Rafe turned to Joe. ''Why are you following us?''

''Thought I might pick up the stalker.'' The restaurant's neon sign reflected off Joe's glasses. ''While I didn't see anything suspicious, I have dug out some interesting information.''

Rhianna's stomach rumbled. ''Why don't we discuss it over dinner?'' Her plan was threefold: to eat, to listen to Joe and to keep the evening from becoming too cozy between her and Rafe. A third person would keep the conversation impersonal and allow her to maintain an emotional distance.

After they'd settled at a table and given their orders

to a waitress, Joe pulled a file from his briefcase. "Duncan Phillips made a bundle in the stock market—"

"Tell us something we don't know." Her patience shot, Rhianna kicked off her shoes beneath the table. Her feet ached. Her stomach made noisy slurping sounds, and the day had been a waste. She'd done no work, missed her animal husbandry class, missed helping her dad with Sweetness. And for what? So she and Rafe could run around playing detective? So she could have her heart broken by Rafe?

"Duncan Phillips has the reputation of a shark. He swam in murky waters and came out clean, but his ex-partner now resides in a federal penitentiary. According to the partner, he took the rap for Duncan's indiscretions."

"What'd they do?" Rafe asked as he calmly reached down and placed Rhianna's foot in his lap. He proceeded to rub her aching arch beneath the table, and as his knowledgeable fingers worked out kinks and cramps, she could barely hold back a tiny moan of pleasure.

"Racketeering."

"What's that?" Rhianna asked.

"Mostly white-collar crimes," Rafe told her, then looked pointedly at the file. "Anything of a violent nature in there?"

"Duncan had a girlfriend in college who was raped and murdered. Duncan was cleared of all charges," Joe told them.

"He told me the story months ago. What else did you find?" Rhianna prodded, almost purring as Rafe rubbed the ball of her foot. Lord, the man had great hands. Slow hands. A lover's hands. At the thought, she yanked her foot away and lowered it to the floor. Rafe simply picked up her other foot and started all over.

Joe frowned. "I don't like loose ends. The police never found the woman's murderer."

Rafe's hands didn't miss a stroke. "I assume the police questioned Duncan Phillips?"

"Duncan didn't have an alibi, but the cops didn't have enough evidence to charge him, either."

"He didn't tell me that! Anything else?" Rhianna sipped her milk, considering the new information again in a new light. She'd never seen Duncan turn violent, but she had seen his temper. When a horse he'd been riding refused a jump, he'd dug his heels into its ribs and cursed long and hard. The horse threw him, and after Duncan regained his feet, he'd struck the horse once with his crop. But that didn't make him a murderer.

"Nothing else on Duncan Phillips." Joe switched to another file as the food arrived.

Rafe excused himself to wash his hands. And Rhianna dug into her steak. "How'd you find out that information about Duncan?"

Joe sipped his water. "One call to his college roommate, another to a business associate did the trick. Then I checked the information with the police."

"Impressive. You work fast. And still have time to tail us, too."

"We'll keep digging."

When Rafe returned, Rhianna had finished half her

steak. She mashed butter into her sweet potato. "So what else did you find?"

"Judge Stuart has ties to the criminal world. He could easily pay someone to stalk Rhianna."

Rafe spread his napkin over his lap. "But why?"

"I don't know. But his ex-wife, Karen, took out a restraining order against him. She claimed he harassed her."

Rhianna paused. She'd thought she'd known Duncan, and while he'd told her about his past, she really hadn't known him at all. He'd never told her the police had questioned him about the murder. And who would have thought that Judge Stuart's wife was afraid of him? Maybe one person couldn't ever really know another. She recalled that wonderful night with Rafe and how hopeful she'd been that he would want to come back to her.

What didn't she know about Rafe? Under that glossy black hair and behind that devastating charm, what secrets lurked? Had another woman jilted him so badly he couldn't open his heart? Maybe he didn't have the capacity to love. Or maybe she just wasn't the right woman.

Damn the man for walking back into her life, disrupting her routine. She didn't need to speculate over what could never be. He didn't want her. And it was time to grow up. Get over him.

"Does everyone have these kinds of secrets?" she wondered aloud.

Rafe pinned her with a stare, but his eyes twinkled. "Do you have secrets, Rhianna? Something you haven't told us?"

His tone might be teasing, but Rhianna didn't like

the way her heart speeded up. This light, intriguing
side of Rafe had always been irresistible to her.

She ignored his question and eyed the third folder,
along with Rafe's coleslaw. "What did you discover
about the Stones?"

Joe shoved his chair back from the table. "Nothing
terrible."

"You sound disappointed," Rhianna commented,
preferring to ignore Rafe's probing gaze as he calmly
passed her his coleslaw.

"They seem to be exactly who they appear to be.
A couple devoted to one another. A rich older man
and his young, loving wife."

Rhianna polished off Rafe's coleslaw in four bites.
"Do I hear a note of sarcasm?"

Joe shrugged. "Let's just say I'm always suspicious when the man is rich and the woman is beautiful. But if you're asking if I have anything solid, I
don't."

Rafe nodded. "Hal and Janet Stone are at their
ranch just outside Highview. We'll pay them a visit
soon."

RAFE DIDN'T WANT TO TAKE Rhianna back to the hotel—not since her stalker had already traced her there
and likely knew that Rafe had reserved a suite for the
night. Thinking hard, he started the car's engine and
adjusted the heat to take the slight chill out of the air,
but he didn't shift into drive. "We shouldn't return
to the hotel."

"And I suppose going home is still out of the question," Rhianna said softly. She patted her rounded

stomach lovingly. "My folks agree we need to keep the baby safe."

Grateful she no longer seemed argumentative, Rafe placed his hand over hers. "If we flew on the senator's private plane, we could be in Highview within the hour."

Rhianna shook her head. "That wouldn't be smart. I shouldn't fly this close to my due date. And since that's your usual mode of transportation, the stalker might expect us to do just that."

"We could drive," Rafe suggested.

Rhianna moved his hand over her stomach, letting him feel his child's kicks. Rafe marveled at the miracle of his son or daughter growing inside Rhianna's womb. A strong surge of protectiveness washed through him, followed by a wave of anger. Who wanted to harm Rhianna and his child? And why?

Rhianna rested her head on the seat back. "Look, whoever is after me also knows I'm with you. Won't he expect you to take me back to the Sutton ranch?"

"Even if he does, I can protect you and the baby there better than anywhere else. Your dad can pick up your truck and I'll have the hotel send our clothes to the ranch. Strangers are noticed in Highview, and Sheriff Noel Demory is a good friend of the family. We also can ask the ranch hands to patrol the grounds."

Rhianna let out a long, low sigh. "I don't know, Rafe. I'm so tired. Do what you think is best." She shifted in her seat and looked him full in the face. In the streetlight's glow, her eyes looked huge, her face pale. Then, as if shaking off her weariness, she hardened her tone. "But if there's any sign of pursuit, I'm not promising to stay put like a sitting duck while everyone gathers round to protect me.''

As if she'd have a choice. Rafe refrained from grinning. Now that his father and brothers knew the situation, that Rhianna carried Rafe's child and the senator's grandchild, no way would they let her walk away, into danger. The child was a Sutton. And Suttons protected their own.

But Rafe saw no reason to make explanations that could wait until Rhianna and the baby were safe. She'd agreed to come with him, given in more easily than he'd expected. ''How good are you at sleeping in a car?''

''Catnaps are all I can manage when I have to use the bathroom every half hour. If you drive, we'll have to make frequent stops.''

''No problem.'' Rafe shifted the car into first gear. ''Use my cell phone and call your parents. We don't want them to worry.''

While Rhianna called, Rafe drove around the block, attempting to spot a tail. He changed directions several times before heading for the highway, and although he never spotted anything suspicious, he still felt as if someone was watching him.

Hoping the feeling would vanish once he reached the ranch, Rafe planned to drive straight through, stopping only when necessary. He let the tension hum through him, keeping him awake, alert and ready for trouble. But nothing happened.

Rhianna closed her eyes and napped, but she kept muttering in her sleep and jerking awake. Between the stresses of pregnancy and the stalker, it was a wonder she dared to shut her eyes at all.

Rafe concentrated on shifting smoothly and merging onto the highway, while frequently glancing in his rearview mirror. He'd driven only a few miles when Rhianna tapped his arm. "Sorry. I need a bathroom break."

"Next exit," he promised. "And there's no need to apologize."

"Thanks."

The walls of the car enclosed them in a cocoon of privacy. And suddenly a different kind of tension filled the air. Rafe didn't know why, but the silence seemed strained and awkward. For once they weren't fighting, but now the darkness seemed fraught with unseen dangers. Maybe it was the politeness between them. He actually felt more comfortable when they were arguing. He flicked on the radio, but even soft jazz didn't take the edge off.

Rafe searched for a safe topic. "Have you thought about a name for the baby?"

"Its last name will be McCloud."

At Rhianna's statement, anger pricked at him. His child should have his name, his heritage. His child should have the same last name as his cousins, the same name as his grandfather. And Rafe suddenly realized he couldn't have picked a more volatile subject.

Sensing that Rhianna would jump all over whatever he said next, Rafe chose to say nothing at all. But he stewed in his own mix of stubbornness, pride and reason. Rhianna didn't expect him to claim their child. She intended to raise the baby alone. And it would be easier for her if the child had the same name as its mother. On one level Rafe understood. On another, every cell in him rebelled.

He hadn't planned for this child. He might not be ready to settle into family life. But he couldn't turn his back on his own blood and pretend the child meant nothing to him. He couldn't pretend the child didn't exist.

Damn it. Even if he asked Rhianna to marry him, he already knew she'd say no. She'd thought he was proposing when she'd seen that jewelry box, and her voice had been firm in her refusal.

Possibly they could reach a solution of joint custody. But what kind of life would that be for his child? Going back and forth between two families, two homes, two worlds. It happened to kids all the time, he told himself. Parents divorced. Kids survived.

Rafe had grown up without a mother. She'd died when he was a child. And he'd always resented her absence. His mother hadn't left him on purpose, but still the painful feeling of abandonment haunted Rafe. He wouldn't forsake his child—financially, physically or emotionally.

Already he'd bonded with the life he'd felt kicking beneath his hand. And those ties would only grow stronger after the baby's birth. Maybe Rhianna would move to Highview, and agree to a joint custody arrangement. He could set her up in a house in town, where she wouldn't have to work, and he could visit without disrupting his child's life.

And have your son or daughter called illegitimate? Children could be so cruel.

Rafe was still sorting through possibilities as he pulled off the highway and headed toward a gas station. He did take a moment to check if any car was following them, but didn't notice one.

He parked by the gas pump and walked around the car and opened Rhianna's door. Her face was devoid of emotion, and he suspected she was hiding her upset over his long silence. He'd thought it better to wait to discuss possibilities, but perhaps he'd been wrong. She needed a measure of certainty in her life. Some statement from him that he wouldn't try to take the child from her. Not knowing what to say, he opened his mouth to speak, but she didn't give him a chance, grabbing her purse and looking around for the bathroom.

He ached to gather her into his arms, but didn't know how when she was as stiff and prickly as a porcupine. As if oblivious to his feelings, she started toward the building. "I won't be long. Do you want anything to drink?"

"No, thanks. And I'm coming with you." He walked by her side, needing the time to clear his head. *And think.*

Rafe wouldn't make promises he couldn't keep. He'd gone through life without entanglements by keeping his relationships simple, easy and casual. The baby had changed everything—his way of thinking, his easygoing attitude. The future could no longer be left to take care of itself.

Rhianna walked into the ladies' room. Ten minutes later, he'd bought her snacks and a drink. When she hadn't returned, he vowed to give her five more minutes.

But he couldn't wait that long. He told himself she just needed air—like when she'd gone out of the restaurant. But maybe she needed help. Maybe her contractions had started early. She'd seemed so tired, almost listless. Weren't those early signs of labor? His sister-in-law Laura had cleaned the house from top to bottom before she'd delivered her second baby. His brother Chase had been furious to see her expending energy cleaning instead of saving her strength for labor. But Laura had been fine.

So why did Rafe's pulse race from just covering the few yards to the ladies' room? He scoured the hallway and the small café. It would be just like Rhianna to slip away for a burger and fries. But she wasn't there. Could he have missed her? He looked behind him but she wasn't browsing the soft drink or candy isle. Finally Rafe knocked on the ladies' room door.

A blonde exited, a look of annoyance on her face. Then she got a good look at Rafe and smiled. "Can I help you?"

"I'm looking for a woman."

"Will anyone do?"

Rafe wanted to barge past the woman into the ladies' room, but restrained his impatience. Flirtation with a stranger was the last thing on his mind, but he used the woman's interest for his own purposes and didn't feel one whit of guilt. "I'm looking for a redhead."

The woman tossed her ponytail. "Blondes have more fun."

"She's eight and a half months pregnant."

"Why are all the good ones already taken?"

"Look, she might be in labor. Could you check and see if she's okay in there?"

"Sure, sugar."

The woman retreated into the rest room. Rafe tapped his boot on the floor and counted to ten.

The blonde returned before he reached five. "She's not there. Maybe—"

Rafe pushed inside. "Rhianna?"

A lady with a small child gasped and walked around Rafe, avoiding him as if he'd escaped from prison. Rafe checked four stalls. Empty.

He rushed outside and searched for a back exit. There. To his left.

Rhianna would be standing outside breathing in the night air, chiding him for his worry. He couldn't wait to hear her teasing him, couldn't wait to hear her tell him not to worry like a mother hen, couldn't wait to hear her demand room to breathe.

Rafe opened the exit door to darkness and the rotting stench of garbage that had sat too long in the sun. Surely Rhianna wouldn't stay out here?

Still he called her name. He walked around the garbage bin and heard a small cry—like an injured animal.

Rafe rounded the building and a cat meowed at his feet and took off for the woods. He saw no sign of Rhianna, and a light sweat broke out along his scalp. She hadn't wanted to live with him and she'd given in to his plan so easily—he now wondered if her agreement had been a ruse. Had she taken off at the first opportunity? Maybe hitched a ride with one of the truckers who had parked out back?

Or had something more sinister happened? Rafe had a bad feeling in his stomach. He searched the store again, went back to the car to see if he'd somehow missed her. But Rhianna was gone. No one in the store had seen her.

Rafe took little comfort in the fact that Rhianna still had her gun in her pocket. While he debated his next move, he prayed she would keep her head and not try anything foolish. If he called the cops and reported her missing, they wouldn't even fill out a missing person's report for twenty-four hours. But they'd keep Rafe here with questions he couldn't answer, when he might be doing something more useful. But what?

Rafe took a flashlight from his car and searched the woods behind the store. He sensed Rhianna was long gone, but he didn't want to leave without checking every possibility. A half hour later, he returned to his car, discouraged and more worried than he'd ever been in his life.

A white piece of paper beneath his windshield wipers made him break into a run. Had Rhianna left him a note?

He ripped the paper from the window and held it to the light. The note wasn't from Rhianna, and his rising hopes drowned in a black sea of horror.

Someone had taken her from him. Fury and anger and fear lashed at Rafe so that his hands shook and he could barely read the message.

Neatly typed, the note held instructions for Rafe. As he read the cold words, icy fear wound up his spine and froze his heart. "If you follow these instructions exactly, Rhianna and your child will live. Do not call law enforcement. Go to the Sutton ranch and raise a ransom. Wait to be contacted."

Rafe blinked at the astronomical amount of money the stalker had demanded. The Suttons didn't have that kind of cash. Their wealth resided in land and cattle.

With a sick feeling, he slumped in his car seat and pulled out his cell phone. There was no question whether or not he would comply. The lives of Rhianna and his child were at stake.

The note hadn't told him he couldn't contact his family. And to raise this kind of money, he needed help.

RHIANNA LAY BOUND hand and foot, gagged and blindfolded, in the back of some kind of vehicle—a big truck, she guessed from the roar of the engine. She fought back tears, determined to keep her air passages free and the terror at bay.

The moment she'd left the stall of the ladies' room, a gun had pressed into her side. Simultaneously, a black hood had dropped over her head. She'd had no time to shout, no time to pull her gun, no time to run. She'd been caught as easily as a lassoed foal. And felt twice as foolish.

She should have been more careful. She shouldn't have let Rafe make all the decisions. Their movements had been too predictable. But she'd been so tired. And she'd been weary of putting up a brave front, tired of fighting Rafe and her own feelings, too.

Seeing Rafe again had been harder than she'd expected. Maybe if she'd prepared herself mentally, she would have been stronger. But he'd come back so unexpectedly that dealing with him, the pregnancy and the stalker had almost overwhelmed her. Even now her thoughts were jumbled and she had trouble focusing. Instead her mind seemed to jump randomly from thought to thought, as if she had little control over her own ideas.

But somehow she would make it through. Although her stalker hadn't found her gun, she couldn't reach it with her hands tied behind her. Already her wrists ached. Her mouth was dry and sore from the gag. She had no way to estimate the time, but sensed too much had passed for any immediate rescue.

By the time Rafe noticed she was missing, she'd be long gone. She thought she was heading south, if her blindfold hadn't altered her sense of direction. She tried to focus on details to push back the terror. She'd never seen her kidnapper's face and held on to the fact that if he didn't want her to see him, then maybe he intended to eventually let her go free. She didn't try to remove the blindfold, had long ago given up on freeing her wrists.

Instead, she told herself she need only wait, stay calm. Keep her head.

Rafe would do everything he could to find her. She took comfort that he wouldn't give up, that no matter the danger or personal cost to himself, he would come after his child. And she held on to that fact to steady her nerves.

Whoever had taken her had handled her gently. She hadn't been shoved or pushed. She guessed she was lying on a mattress. Surely no one would go to such trouble only to kill her?

A twinge in her stomach caused Rhianna to shift slightly. She lay on her side and wished she could rub the aching spot. But the twinge stopped by itself and she let her thoughts drift. To Rafe. She would never forget the look on his face when he'd felt the baby kick, the wonder in his eyes, the pride and love in his expression.

Her stomach jerked, contracted.

God, no. Not now.

She breathed deeply, willing herself to relax.

She waited, willing her stomach not to tense up again. But all the will in the world couldn't hold back nature.

Suddenly Rhianna had another problem. Her contractions had begun.

Chapter Six

The Sutton family gathered at the senator's house in the library, and Rafe appreciated the concern he read in his brothers' faces. The Sutton sons resembled one another with their dark hair and gray eyes, but none of them would ever be mistaken for twins. Tyler, his eldest brother, who ran the vast Sutton ranch, walked with a cane and a slight limp. Dr. Cameron Sutton, the gentlest and the most kind-hearted, was the size of a mountain man, while Chase had the weathered skin and crinkled eyes of a rancher. Unlike his brothers, Rafe was whipcord lean. He matched Cameron in height, but gave up a good fifty pounds to him. But more important than physical characteristics was the mental toughness and support the family lent to Rafe. Even his sisters-in-law, Laura and Alexa, were solid, strong women who had survived trouble while maintaining loving natures.

Laura rocked a sleeping baby in her arms, while her eldest son, Keith, and Cameron's three-year-old genius twins, Flynn and Jason, quietly played video games in a corner. If the twins stayed out of trouble for more than ten minutes, they might set a new good-behavior record. Luckily, they were as good at getting out of trouble as they were at finding it.

The senator finished pouring drinks and settled by the huge fireplace. "Rafe, I don't have that kind of cash—"

"We do." Jason, wise beyond his three years, put down his video game.

When Jason moved to the center of the room, Flynn was right beside him. The two boys often disagreed, but this time they'd come to an understanding. And the offer was genuine. The boys had a vast inheritance waiting for them when they turned eighteen—a gift from a great-grandfather.

Flynn nodded solemnly. "You can have our trust fund, Uncle Rafe."

"I can't take your money, boys, but I appreciate the offer." Rafe hugged each of them while a lump formed in his throat at the twins' generosity. They might be sixty pounds of pure trouble, but their hearts were solid gold.

Cameron looked at his boys with pride. "I'm proud of you boys for making the offer."

"We want to help," Flynn said simply.

"You just did," Rafe told them.

Flynn frowned. "How?"

"By making me feel better. By reminding me I'm not alone with my trouble."

"We can't use the boys' trust, not even for collateral," Alexa Sutton, Cameron's wife, added. "I checked with the trustees, and they won't let us risk it."

The senator pulled the twins onto his lap, and Keith settled at his feet. "As I was saying, we may not have cash, but the land is free and clear. I've already spoken to the bank. If we all sign the note, we should be able to borrow the money.''

Rafe paced, unable to hold still. Since he'd read the kidnapper's note, he'd been unable to eat or to sleep or to keep his pulse from racing like a runaway bull. And his father's news didn't set his mind at ease. In the past few years, the senator had divided the vast ranch, giving equal shares to each brother. Rafe supposed Chase and Laura would manage, since they would eventually inherit her family's ranch. Cameron would be okay, as he made his living as a doctor. Rafe could practice law if necessary, but this place was all Tyler knew. Although his brother could work as a foreman on any ranch, it wouldn't be the same as owning his own place, a place that had been passed from father to son. A place where Suttons came to rebuild their lives, lick their wounds; a place that was safe from outsiders; a place where the family stuck together, loved and prospered.

Their father may have divided up the acreage, but the Suttons still ran the operation as one unit. Rafe didn't want his brothers and their families to forfeit their heritage. Once they mortgaged the land, the bank payments would be astronomical. They'd be lucky not to lose everything. And yet he couldn't see another option.

''I'll never be able to pay you all back.''

Chase took Laura's hand, and she nodded in agreement as Chase spoke for both of them. ''You would do the same for any of us.''

''I don't know what to say.''

''There's nothing *to* say.'' Tyler set aside his cane

and raised his glass to Rafe. "Rhianna and your child's life are at risk and worth more than cattle and land."

Chase lifted Keith into his arms. "Besides, Dad paid off the land once. We can do it again."

"Beef prices are at an all-time high. People are eating meat again thanks to those high-protein diet books." Tyler crossed one ankle over the other and stared out the window. "I'll start making arrangements for auction. We'll do an early roundup."

The phone rang and the senator checked his caller ID. "The number is blocked." Raising his eyebrows he answered the phone. "Yes?"

Rafe noted the tension in his father's tone. So did his brothers, and the room stilled until they could have heard a penny drop. Not much shook his father, and as his face paled, Rafe's pulse raced. "Rhianna?"

His father set down the phone. "That was her kidnapper. Rhianna's in labor."

"Holy s—" Rafe remembered the presence of children in the room barely in time. "Rhianna's not due for another two weeks. What else did they say? Is she all right? When will they release her?"

"As soon as we have the money, we're supposed to announce it over the ranch's radio."

Every hand carried a radio tuned to the ranch's frequency. The radios didn't always work, but they usually helped keep the hands in touch. That meant the kidnapper was close by. Perhaps they could find him before… No, Rafe wouldn't risk two lives trying to play hero.

The senator picked up the phone and dialed his banker. Several minutes later, he put the phone back in the cradle, his face grave. "The bank wants an up-to-date appraisal—"

Rafe gritted his teeth. "That'll take weeks!"

"—and a profit and loss statement from a certified public accountant. Then the board has to vote...."

Cameron rubbed his forehead. "First babies are notoriously slow to arrive, but Rhianna doesn't have that long."

RHIANNA CONCENTRATED ON breathing during the painful contraction as a man freed her ankles and took her, still blindfolded, from the vehicle. At least she assumed it was a man, since he never spoke, just pressed a gun into her back.

She didn't hear any cars going by, and breathed in the scent of pine. Then she was placed in a musty-smelling room and someone untied her hands, but her wrists were too numb for her to go for the gun in her pocket. The door slammed shut and she heard hammering. Then silence. By the time she could feel her hands again and had removed the gag and hood, she was alone, in darkness. She explored her new surroundings by touch after the latest contraction had passed. The building's windows were boarded up from the outside. She did find a small bathroom and made use of it. After she performed the necessities, she washed her hands and rinsed her mouth, then left to explore her prison.

The door she'd come in through was locked. She debated trying to shoot the lock or hinges, but feared a ricochet could hurt her or the baby. And she had no clue if anyone guarded the door from the other side.

No way could she dig through the concrete floor. And there was no way to signal for help.

She bumped into a cot with a small refrigerator beside it. Groping inside the fridge, she found several sandwiches, but just drinking a sip from one of the water bottles made her nauseous. She felt along the walls, but never found a light switch.

A contraction cut short her explorations, and she sat down hard on the cot. She panted and rubbed her back until the contraction ceased, then she stood again.

She explored her ten-by-ten-foot cell and quickly realized that even if she escaped, she was in no condition to run. Not with contractions coming every ten to fifteen minutes and lasting about thirty seconds.

The thought of delivering the baby alone sent shivers down her spine. How could she be clammy and hot and yet cold at the same time?

To conserve her strength, she lay back on the cot. For courage, she removed the gun and kept it next to her side, but hidden beneath the blanket. She had no idea if someone came back during one of her contractions whether she'd have the strength to steady the gun and shoot.

But she vowed to try. And then another pain took over, this contraction stronger, harder and so painful she doubled over on the bed.

Sweet Jesus! She'd expected pain, but not the agony of back labor. The small of her back felt as if an ice pick stabbed her. The contraction seemed to take forever. She wanted her mother, her doctor. She wanted Rafe.

She didn't want to deliver his baby alone, in this

godforsaken spot. She didn't want to have to be brave. She wanted to be surrounded by modern medicine and people who cared about her. She wanted to feel safe.

As the contraction eased, the pain disappeared completely. But she knew it would return. And she didn't know how much more she could take. Rhianna rolled to her side and saved her strength, unaware of the tears sliding down her cheeks.

RHIANNA WAS IN LABOR. And held hostage by a kidnapper. Fury surged through Rafe, raw, scalding fury that made him want to strike out at whoever would do this to her, slam him into a wall. It took all his restraint to keep his voice even. "We don't have time for the bank to lend us the ransom."

The senator nodded, his face grave. "Then we go to plan B."

"We call in law enforcement?" Tyler asked.

Rafe shook his head and paced. "Surely you don't want to bluff and pretend we have the money? I won't risk their lives."

The senator put his pipe in his mouth, but he didn't light it. "We'll go to Judge Stuart."

"Where would he come by that kind of money?" Rafe asked with a frown.

"He's involved in real estate transactions throughout the state."

"But will he lend it to us?" Rafe asked.

The senator's eyes narrowed in thought. "Several years back, meat prices were down and we were strapped. He offered to buy half the ranch or float us a loan. Let me see what I can do."

The family exited the room while the senator made his phone call. Meanwhile, Rafe phoned the detective he'd hired and filled him in on the latest developments. "Try and make the exchange for Rhianna at the same time you turn over the money."

"I may not have a choice," Rafe told him.

"Put the money in the two reinforced army duffel bags I'll send you," the detective suggested. "The senator should have the bank show him how to mark the bills. We'll place a bug inside the bags' lining so that after the exchange we can track the kidnapper."

"How fast can you deliver the duffel bags?" Rafe asked.

"Faster than you'll get and mark the cash," the detective promised.

Rafe hung up the phone as his father joined him and signaled a thumbs-up. "Stuart agreed. His attorney will have the papers drawn up within the hour."

"How long before we have the cash?" Rafe asked, knowing every minute counted.

"We had to draw on a Denver bank. It'll take two, maybe three hours before we're set."

While he paced and looked out the window, Rafe asked his father to have the bank mark the bills. But his main concern was Rhianna. "Dad, what if the kidnappers don't call back? What if she has that baby all by herself?"

The senator shook his head. Clearly he couldn't answer Rafe's questions. "Whoever took Rhianna is slick. Judge Stuart arranged for guards to accompany him with the cash."

The next three hours seemed to take years. Judge Stuart arrived with the cash, and Rafe had word put out over the radio to the kidnappers as instructed. He stashed the money into the duffel bags while everyone signed papers. Their attorney had sent over a notary, so the loan would be legal and the mortgage and note would be recorded in the courthouse.

Tense from all the waiting, Rafe tucked his fully charged cell phone into his pocket and waited some more. While the judge and his father shook hands, Rafe's cell phone rang.

He heard a mechanical voice say, "Take the money and drive into Highview. Go alone."

Rafe picked up the duffel bags and headed toward the front door, where his father and the judge waited. "I'm supposed to go into Highview."

"Are you armed?" Judge Stuart asked.

Rafe shook his head.

"Good."

His father agreed. "Just follow the instructions and don't try to be a hero."

"That's the plan." Rafe only hoped he would arrive to find Rhianna well.

Cameron met him at his car. He placed a black backpack on the seat next to Rafe. "Rhianna is probably still in labor. She'll be scared, which will make the pain seem worse. Many women turn irrational when they reach transition—the last stage before they deliver. Don't worry if she's a little out of her head. Just get her to the hospital."

"So what's in the backpack?" Rafe asked.

"Some stuff you might need." Cameron clapped him on the back. "Remember, I'm just a phone call away."

Rafe drove toward Highview, and just before he hit

town, his phone rang again. The mechanical voice instructed, ''Get on the next train heading south.''

Before he could ask to speak to Rhianna, before he could say a word, the phone went dead. Rafe drove straight to the train station and bought a ticket. He slung Cameron's backpack over his shoulder and then picked up the two heavy duffels.

As the train chugged out of Highview, Rafe worried. The next stop wouldn't be for half an hour. Rhianna had been in labor almost all day. How much longer could she wait?

RHIANNA WIPED THE SWEAT off her brow with the back of her hand. The last contraction had been the worst. She'd given up praying for help, given up wondering how long the pains could last. Her body had taken over, the contractions coming stronger, faster.

She tried to pant through the pain. Her lips grew dry and her feet felt like blocks of ice. But her body broke into a light sweat.

At least she knew the baby had turned. During her last checkup, her obstetrician had told her the baby's head was down, already aligned to come out.

Rhianna had long since passed the point of hoping the labor would stop. The baby wanted out. Rhianna wanted the baby out. And yet she felt absolutely no urge to push. So she didn't. She'd seen enough horses born to know her body would tell her when the time was right.

Light-headed, she sipped the water she'd placed beside the cot, kicked off her panties, groaned as another contraction clenched her stomach.

Breathe.

Breathe.
Breathe.

Rhianna told herself the contraction was just like the last. She'd gotten through that one and she'd get through this one.

RAFE FOLLOWED HIS LATEST instructions with sweat beading his forehead and dripping into his eyes. He carried the heavy duffel bags to the last car of the train, opening the car door and stepping onto the windy platform of the caboose as he'd been ordered.

A truck with no license plate and a masked driver drove along a dirt road next to the train. Rafe's instructions were to throw the duffel bags into the truck. Then he'd be told where to find Rhianna.

Rafe didn't like it. After he paid the ransom, the kidnapper had no reason to let Rhianna go. But Rafe didn't think about backing out.

With two heaves, he tossed the bags into the pickup's open bed. The driver immediately shot away from the road, and Rafe wondered if the kidnapper would uphold his end of the bargain.

Was Rhianna still alive? Rafe didn't know, and the uncertainty had him clawing leather. Only once before in his life had he been this scared—when he'd been a child and his mother had died. His mother hadn't been much older than Rhianna—too young to collapse on the kitchen floor, too young to leave her sons to grow up without her.

Rafe's mouth was so dry he couldn't swallow. He stared at the phone in his hand and willed it to ring. Ten minutes later, he got a call and, with shaking hands, stepped back into the car, out of the wind, to answer.

The mechanical voice he hated said, "Rhianna is locked in Hal and Janet Stone's old guest cabin."

A measure of relief that the stalker had kept his end of the bargain mixed with worry about how Rafe could help Rhianna. Hal and Janet were still in Denver, so he couldn't call them. It'd take the senator and Cameron or the cops an hour to reach the Stones' ranch due to switchbacks in the mountain roads.

If Rafe waited for the train to stop, he'd still have to rent a car and drive back. He'd lose an hour and a half—maybe two.

But the train was passing by the Stones' ranch right now. He could be with Rhianna within minutes.

All he had to do was jump.

RAFE STOOD ON THE CABOOSE platform. Wind whipped his hair and he lurched from foot to foot in impatience, waiting for the train to slow on an uphill section. He took several deep breaths as he watched for a spot free of boulders and trees.

Then he leaped from the speeding train. He took the brunt of the fall on his feet but didn't try to maintain his balance. Instead he rolled, letting the momentum absorb the shock of his fall, grateful the backpack protected his spine.

He tumbled and somersaulted down the steep grade. His shoulder struck a rock, the impact knocking the wind out of him. But as his lungs started to pump again, he moved his arms and legs. Everything worked, and grateful he hadn't suffered anything more serious than a few bumps and bruises, he pushed to his feet.

Rafe backtracked to the dirt road and then followed the dusty path to the Stones' property. Although he suspected the kidnappers would be long gone, he still kept a wary eye out. But he saw nothing except a white-tailed deer, cattle and an eagle circling high overhead. A glance at the sun told him he had another hour, hour and a half of daylight left.

Rafe shifted the pack that Cameron had given him and took out the cell phone. He called his father, who promised to send help, but Rafe knew he couldn't expect anyone from the Sutton ranch to reach him for at least an hour.

Luckily, he'd visited the Stones many times and knew exactly where Rhianna was being held. He by-passed the main house and the barn and headed directly to the old cabin that had once been Hal's bachelor pad.

Rafe ran the last mile and arrived out of breath and more worried than ever. The door and windows were covered with nailed planks from the outside—to keep out kids. Or to keep Rhianna a prisoner?

Heart pounding, Rafe pried a board loose from over the front door. He shoved the door open with his shoulder and stepped inside. ''Rhianna?''

''Get out!'' she screamed, and then followed with a groan and a gasped whimper.

She sounded out of control and tortured, and her moan of pain made him fearful for her health. Rafe's eyes hadn't adjusted to the darkness. He couldn't see inside the room. ''It's Rafe. Are you okay?''

When she let out another low moan of pain, Rafe

rushed forward. He bumped into a chair and swore under his breath, but kept moving toward Rhianna, who was panting in a loud, steady rhythm.

Rafe couldn't see a damn thing. Didn't want to leave her side, but couldn't help her in the darkness. ''I'll be right back.''

She just kept panting.

He ran outside and pried plywood off two windows. He rushed inside once more to find her lying quietly on her side.

Kneeling beside her, he smoothed damp hair off her forehead. ''We need to get you to the hospital.''

''I don't...think...there's time. Contractions are—'' She gasped. Started panting again. Grabbed his hand and squeezed so hard he thought she might break the bones, but he didn't pull away.

With his free hand, he yanked out the cell phone and called Cameron who picked up on the first ring.

''How far apart are the contractions?'' his brother asked calmly.

''A minute—no more.''

''Has her water broken?'' Cam asked.

''I don't know. I just got here.''

Rhianna let out another low moan. Rafe shuddered, wishing he could take the pain away. He wedged the cell phone between ear and shoulder, slid the pack off his back with his free hand and yanked on the zipper. ''Is there anything you gave me that will help her with the pain?''

''Yes. But I'd rather you didn't give it to her unless absolutely necessary. An anesthetic can slow the labor, and that isn't good for the mother or baby.''

Rafe's heartbeat seemed to echo in his ears with

every labored breath Rhianna drew. "What can I do?"

"Keep her calm, encourage her."

"What else?"

"You need to calm down, too."

"Easy for you to say."

"Most babies don't need any help. The main thing is to keep Rhianna and the baby clean and comfortable."

Rhianna let out a low scream.

Rafe squeezed her hand and kept his tone low. "You're doing fine."

"I'm…not…fine!" Rhianna panted. She was having little rest between contractions.

Over the phone, Cam's confident voice gave directions in Rafe's ear. "Take the newspapers out of the backpack. Spread them under her. Put more newspapers on the ground or floor and dump the supplies out of the bag onto the paper."

Rafe did as his brother asked, grateful to see baby blankets, towelettes, towels and a clean robe for Rhianna among a bunch of medical supplies. "Now what?"

"I need to push. Can I push?" Rhianna yelled, loudly enough for Cam to hear.

"Tell her not yet. Rinse your hands in alcohol and put on the surgical gloves. Is the baby's head crowning?"

"I can't do five things at once. I'm going to set the phone by Rhianna's ear. Talk to her."

Rafe had no idea what his brother said, but Rhianna seemed to calm a little. Meanwhile, he washed his hands, struggled with the gloves, then spread the newspapers under Rhianna.

Finally he lifted her skirt. "The baby's almost here."

"Duh! No kidding," Rhianna panted, almost whacking him with her foot as she writhed in pain.

He grabbed back the phone. "I can see the baby's head, Cam."

"Tell her to push with the next—"

"Push."

Rhianna grunted. Her face tightened with effort. Rafe moved between her legs. "You're doing fine, sweetheart. The baby's coming. Push!"

"I'm tired."

"Come on, darling. Just one more time," he coaxed.

"I can't do this."

"Yes, you can. You're almost done."

"Open the jar of lubrication," Cam instructed. "Try and ease the baby's head through. Be gentle. Don't force anything."

Rhianna thrashed and Rafe steadied her, grateful for the number of foals and calves he'd helped into this world—otherwise he'd have been too nervous to sound calm when his heart was beating a tattoo against his ribs. "Sweetheart, the baby wants you, needs you. I know you're tired, but soon you'll be holding the baby in your arms. Push."

Rhianna labored. The baby slipped into Rafe's hands and let out a cry.

"I've got it."

"Wipe the nose and mouth. Don't try and cut the umbilical cord. Use the string and tie it tight." Cam

calmly issued orders and Rafe followed them, his
hands shaking with the miracle of life he held.

Tears brimmed in his eyes as gently, carefully, he
wiped the baby clean and wrapped it in a towel, then
placed it on Rhianna's stomach. ''You did it, sweetheart. She's a beautiful baby girl.''

Chapter Seven

Two days later, Rhianna thought she'd regained her strength enough to dress and walk around Rafe's house, but Rafe insisted she stay in bed, even though the doctor at the hospital had told them they'd done a superb job of delivering Allison Joanne.

Rhianna smiled at the eight-pound baby in her arms and thought she might not put her down until she turned five and had to attend kindergarten. She loved the scent of powder and the sweet odor of baby shampoo, marveled over the round pink cheeks, the dark blue eyes hidden by a crescent of inch-long lashes.

Baby Allison snuggled into Rhianna's warmth, her thumb in her mouth, her huge round eyes staring at her mother with curiosity and contentment. Allison may have come into the world with a shout, but she seemed content to stare quietly at Rhianna and bond with her mama, considerately waking her only once during the night for a breast feeding.

Rhianna's heart swelled with protective feelings and love. She'd always known that she and her baby would be close, but until now, she hadn't quite realized the extent of that closeness.

"Knock, knock." Rafe entered the sunny bedroom, his gaze going immediately to the baby, his eyes gleaming with pride. "Laura sent over more baby stuff."

Rhianna looked around the room. Allison already had a cradle, a crib, a high chair, a stroller, a car seat, a playpen and a changing table. The entire Sutton family had brought presents, as had Rhianna's parents. The room overflowed with toys and furniture, so that Rafe had to wind his way through.

"I can't accept any more gifts," Rhianna protested.

"Sure you can." Rafe kissed her forehead and then his daughter's. "She's perfect. Can I hold her?"

"Only if you tell me what's going on."

"What do you mean?"

He knew damn well what she meant. He'd refused to talk about the stalker ever since the baby had been born.

Rafe reached for Allison with an expertise that made Rhianna uncomfortable. Why couldn't he be one of those men who was afraid of babies? Why did his eyes have to soften and his voice turn to a husky murmur every time he held Allison?

"Any leads on the kidnappers?" Rhianna asked. Now that Allison had been born, she was more anxious than ever to solve the problem and return to her home. In just two days, Rafe had become very attached to his daughter. And Allison seemed to respond to Rafe, waving her little fists in excitement whenever he came by—about every fifteen minutes. He seemed as fascinated with the baby as Rhianna.

"That's a good girl. Your uncle Cam says it's good exercise to suck on your thumb."

"But it might make her teeth crooked."

"She doesn't have teeth."

Rhianna handed him the pacifier. "See if you can get her to take this. I haven't had any luck."

Allison turned her head away. "She's stubborn like her mother," Rafe said.

"And good at avoiding things, like her father. Just because I've had a baby doesn't mean my brain's turned off. Did the detective find out who might have—"

"Nope. Sheriff Demory wants to talk to you. He hopes you'll remember some detail that you forgot to tell me."

She sighed in frustration. "I didn't see anything. No one ever spoke one word to me."

"Easy. We'll find whoever's after you."

But when? "What about the money? I overheard the twins say that you put a bug in the duffel bag to track the bad guys."

"The empty duffel bags were dumped about two miles from the train tracks. Another dead end, I'm afraid."

"And what about Janet and Hal Stone? You found me at their place. Surely it can't be a coincidence that they bought jewelry from Biddle and Baines and that I ended up imprisoned on their property?"

Rafe took the baby brush off the dresser and ran it through Allison's curly red hair. "They have an alibi. Both of them were in Denver and have witnesses with impeccable reputations."

"Maybe they hired someone to do their dirty work?" Rhianna suggested.

"It's possible. But what would be the motive?"

"The ransom?"

"But the Stones are already rich. I did ask Janet about her jewelry boxes from Biddle and Baines."

"And?"

"She claims she never saves them."

Despite the covers and the warm robe she was wearing, a sudden chill made Rhianna shiver. "Are you telling me we still have no clue—"

"You'll be safe here." Rafe looked down into his daughter's face, and Rhianna saw the worry clouding his eyes. "We have ranch hands riding the fence line. Sheriff Demory is no slouch. He'll keep his eyes open. And the detective is still digging."

Rhianna could see she would have to drag every detail out of Rafe. "The twins also mentioned that your family had to mortgage the ranch to save us."

Rafe sighed. "Cam and Alexa need to teach those boys when to keep their mouths shut."

Rhianna didn't understand why Rafe was trying to protect her. Didn't he understand that knowing the situation was much better than being kept in the dark? But she didn't argue. Rafe had been so good to her, she'd never forget how tender he'd been while he delivered their child. Without his words of encouragement, she might have panicked. For the past two days, he'd been thoughtful and, if she hadn't known better, she would have believed loving. She had to keep reminding herself that he'd acted to save his daughter—not her.

Still, she didn't want to bicker. "The twins are adorable. And smart. Remind me to thank them for assembling the tricycle Tyler bought for Allison."

"Who gave my sons tools?" Cam walked through

the bedroom door. "And how are you feeling?" he asked Rhianna.

"I'm fine, but Rafe insists on coddling me," she said softly. She liked this brother of Rafe's who'd talked her through a very difficult moment of labor over a telephone. Dr. Cameron Sutton had a solid presence that Rhianna found comforting. She'd always wanted a brother like Cameron.

"The bike came with tools," Tyler admitted as he limped into the crowded bedroom, carefully making his way with his cane. Rhianna liked this quiet brother, too. He carried himself with a certain dignity and his face showed he was a caring man.

"Did you get the hammer and screwdriver back?" Cam asked with a slight raising of his eyebrows.

Tyler scratched his head, his face puzzled. "How much damage could they—"

"Don't worry." Rafe grinned at Cam. "My office is locked. The computer's safe."

A loud crash downstairs made the adults jump.

Chase's raised voice floated up the stairs as he lectured the twins. "Doors tend to fall when one removes the pins."

Cam's eyes twinkled. "I'm assuming no one was hurt or Chase would have already called for help."

"We'll fix it, Uncle Chase," the twins replied. "Rafe locked his office door and we just wanted to prove we could get inside."

Cam made his way out, his voice imperturbable. "I'd better go check out the damage."

Rafe looked at Rhianna and grinned. "Don't worry, Cam, I'll send you a bill."

Tyler held out his arms for Allison, and Rafe reluctantly passed her to him. Rhianna had no qualms about Tyler holding the infant. Rafe's sisters-in-law had trained these men well, and even the unmarried Tyler seemed to enjoy cooing at the baby.

Gently Tyler pulled Allison's thumb out of her mouth and inserted the pacifier. "Thank God we finally got a sweet little girl."

Allison spit the pacifier in Tyler's face. While he jerked back in surprise, Allison calmly put her thumb back in her mouth.

Rhianna and Rafe burst into laughter, but their shared mirth was cut short by the senator. He strode into the room, wearing a suit and tie as if he'd just come from an important meeting. Tyler and Rafe noted their father's solemn expression and their grins died.

"What's wrong, Dad?" Rafe asked.

Tyler handed Allison back to Rhianna. Her daughter gazed at her so trustingly that she had to refrain from hugging her too tightly. The Suttons had been careful to protect Rhianna from problems, but clearly something had occurred that the senator felt she should know about.

Rhianna sat straighter against her pillows. "You don't need to coddle me. The only reason I'm still in bed is because Rafe insists on spoiling me."

The senator took her hand, but his gaze rested on his granddaughter, a fond light in his eyes that reminded her of Rafe. "You deserve to be spoiled." While the elder Sutton clearly had something difficult to say, he seemed to weigh whether she could take the news.

Rafe sat next to her on the bed. "Rhianna's tougher than she looks."

"It's not Rhianna I'm worried about." The senator's gaze moved from the baby to his youngest son, and suddenly Rhianna realized that his concern was for Rafe. But why?

"Rhianna has another visitor downstairs."

Rhianna frowned. Her parents had already come and gone. They couldn't afford to take time off work or away from the horses for very long. But she'd phoned them this morning and all seemed well at home.

Her friends didn't know that she was hiding here. And she'd already met all the Suttons. So who had tracked her to the ranch? And why did the normally unflappable senator seem so worried about his son?

As if steeling himself for bad news, Rafe drew into himself. His eyes took on a quicksilver glint. His shoulders braced and he shoved himself to his feet. "Don't keep us waiting. Who's downstairs?"

"Duncan Phillips."

Tyler let out a low whistle. "Want me to get rid of him?"

Rhianna sighed. "How'd he find out I was here?"

Rafe turned to her, but not quite before he'd hid his worry beneath a sweep of dark lashes. "Obviously, Duncan has his own resources. Do you want to see him?"

"Not particularly." At her instant response, Rafe and the senator shared a long look. The senator's eyes burned with questions. Rafe remained silent. Rhianna shook her head. "The last time I saw Duncan, I thought I made it clear we had nothing more to say to one another.''

The senator's brows rose but his voice remained gentle. ''Men like Duncan don't take no for an answer.''

Rafe shrugged slightly, as if the matter had already been resolved. ''I'll send him away.''

Rhianna tugged on Rafe's hand, stopping him from leaving. ''Maybe I should hear what he has to say.''

''Why?'' Rafe asked.

''The kidnapper knew I was with you. Duncan knows I'm with you. If Duncan is the kidnapper, maybe he'll slip and say something that could help us nail him.''

''I won't leave you alone with him,'' Rafe promised, and she took comfort in his words. ''But you needn't face him unless you're ready.''

Strength and determination surged through Rhianna. She was ready to put this entire incident behind her. She needed to move on with her life. And she'd do whatever she must to protect her daughter and herself.

The senator and Tyler left, and a minute later, Duncan entered her room. He seemed a bit bewildered by the baby things, but strode straight to her side and placed a vase of white roses on her nightstand. Rhianna didn't say a word. She just sat holding her daughter, protected by Rafe's presence, and waited to hear whatever Duncan had to say.

When Duncan turned to Rafe first, somehow she wasn't surprised. Another man might have said something about the baby or congratulated her on the birth.

Duncan always took care of business first. "Could we have some privacy?"

Rafe folded his arms across his chest. "I'm afraid that's not possible right now."

Duncan hadn't reached the pinnacle of success in his career without the ability to read men. Clearly Rafe didn't intend to budge from her room. Accepting he had no control over the situation, Duncan simply made the best of the opportunity he'd been given. "I see." With that he turned his back on Rafe and spoke softly to Rhianna. "I'm sorry we quarreled."

"We didn't just have a little spat, Duncan. You called me a thief in front of my family and friends."

"I was upset. That night you wouldn't look at me, you only had eyes for Rafe."

Had she been that obvious? Had Duncan lashed out at her because he'd been hurt? But she'd already turned down his marriage proposal at that point. Suddenly she recalled the senator's opinion about how men like Duncan didn't take no for an answer. Maybe he'd thought she'd been playing a game. Maybe he'd become unglued by not getting what he wanted. Had he really not understood she'd been serious about her refusal?

Duncan suddenly dropped to one knee beside her bed. He dug into his pocket and pulled out a jewelry box from Biddle and Baines. He opened the box and the same obscenely large diamond he'd offered her before winked at her. "Marry me, Rhianna. I love you."

"I'm sorry, Duncan." Rhianna looked down at Allison. "I have a daughter now."

"I'll adopt her. We'll find her a nanny. Send her

to the best boarding schools. She needn't interfere with our lives.''

''That's not good enough for my daughter,'' Rafe interrupted softly, but with an edge of steel beneath his words.

''I'm offering more than you are,'' Duncan said, his voice surprisingly reasonable. ''I'll marry her. Make the baby legitimate. Give her my name.''

''She already has a name,'' Rafe murmured, ''Allison Joanne Sutton.''

''Sutton?'' Rhianna couldn't contain her gasp of surprise. Rafe had taken care of the birth certificate while she'd been checked over by the doctor in the hospital. Rafe had known she'd planned to name the baby Allison Joanne McCloud—so mother and daughter would have the same last name. At Rafe's arrogance, her anger blossomed. ''How dare you go against my wishes?''

''She's my daughter,'' Rafe said simply, as if daring her to contest that fact.

''But—''

''It doesn't matter,'' Duncan interrupted. ''Its name can be changed.''

It? Duncan was calling her beautiful little girl *it?* And Rafe, damn him, had made everything more complicated by going against her wishes and naming himself as father on Allison's birth certificate.

Men! Right now Rhianna wanted to scream at both of them. She'd like nothing better that to knock their two stubborn heads together.

But before she could say a word, Duncan stood and faced Rafe. ''Judge Stuart told me you mortgaged the ranch. You could lose everything your family's worked for.''

Rafe's eyes narrowed to two slits of masculine determination. ''We'll make the payments.''

''Maybe. But why struggle? If Rhianna agrees to marry me, then I'll pay off your debt. We'll call it a dowry.''

Rafe cocked his chin at a stubborn angle. ''No. Suttons pay their own debts.''

Duncan ignored Rafe and stood over Rhianna. ''Do you want the Suttons to lose this place because of you? Marry me, Rhianna, and the nightmare will go away.''

Rhianna didn't like Duncan's veiled threats. She didn't like his bullying words delivered in a tone so soft he reminded her of a rattlesnake about to strike. This icy side of Duncan was one she hadn't seen before. He came bearing gifts of diamond rings and flowers, promising to wipe away her debt to the Suttons, but an icy chill stole over her heart. Duncan didn't love her. He just didn't like to lose. She wondered if he was capable of love.

She wouldn't accept his proposal. And yet he'd said the Suttons might not be able to repay the loan. Her refusal could cost Rafe's family all they held dear, their legacy.

Duncan took her hand, and she felt nothing. ''I'll give you a month, Rhianna. One month to become my bride.''

She didn't answer. Couldn't say a word. Her throat clogged over the huge lump of anger there.

Rafe stepped between Duncan and Rhianna. He snapped the jewelry box shut and stuffed it into Duncan's front pocket. "I believe you've overstayed your welcome. But would you mind telling me where the jewelry box came from?"

"I ordered another to replace the one I crushed."

Duncan walked out the door, speaking over his shoulder. "Come to me soon, Rhianna."

Duncan had given her a lot to think about. His words lingered in her mind for weeks after he was gone.

TWO WEEKS LATER, Rhianna felt back to her old self, if not her old shape. Her shirts were still a bit too tight across the bust and her tummy not quite as tight as before. Yet she didn't mind. How could she when she had a wonderful baby for her efforts?

In just two weeks, Allison had learned to turn her head at the sound of Rhianna's or Rafe's voice. She could hold up her head and look curiously at the world. And her blue eyes had started to darken to Sutton gray.

Rhianna enjoyed taking her on strolls around the house and barn, carrying the baby in a pack, snuggled against her chest. Although she felt safe on Sutton land, Rhianna never traveled farther than shouting distance, keeping Allison's safety in mind.

Duncan may not have been threatening Rhianna during his visit, but she didn't trust him. He'd gone out of his way to pry into her business. And his offer to pay off the Sutton debt if she married him was like some kind of deal made in the Dark Ages. Rhianna wasn't property for men to bargain over.

To Rafe's credit, he'd never mentioned Duncan's offer again. But she knew he worried over his family's ability to repay the loan. Tyler and Rafe had been speaking quietly once, but she'd overheard their plans. Something about an early roundup, cattle prices and selling an art collection.

She hated the position she'd put the Suttons in. Felt guilty that they could lose this wonderful ranch due to her troubles.

Not one of the Suttons had pried into her and Rafe's private affairs. No one had made her feel uncomfortable because she and Rafe weren't married. They'd simply included her because she was the mother of Rafe's child. Their generosity astounded her. Their courage made her want to do everything possible to help. But what could she do?

Rhianna cuddled Allison and walked toward the barn. Several voices pulled her from her deep thoughts.

She looked up as she entered the stable, breathed in the scent of fresh manure, feed and hay. At home she always had to let her eyes adjust to a dimly lit interior. But this stable had high windows to let in sunshine, and she spotted Rafe talking to a man and woman.

As she strolled with the baby down the wide center isle, Rhianna paused and patted several of Rafe's animals, which stuck out curious noses as she passed. Rafe had quite a collection. She admired a pretty sorrel, the mare's freshly groomed coat a rich mahogany red. A spectacular gray with a white blaze on his forehead nickered softly in greeting. She scratched behind his ears but kept walking toward Rafe.

Allison perked up at the sound of her father's

voice. Rafe swore she smiled when she saw him, and Rhianna teased him that it was simply gas.

As Rhianna moved closer, she recognized Janet and Hal Stone. Janet wore designer jeans and a scarlet riding jacket that matched her alligator boots. Hal was dressed more simply in a black studded shirt with silver fringe, and black jeans.

Janet smiled brightly as Rhianna approached with Allison. "Ohh, look at the little darling. May I hold the baby?"

Rhianna eyed Janet's jacket doubtfully. "She just ate. She might spit up...."

"So what?" Janet cooed and reached for Allison. "I adore babies."

Hal rolled his eyes at the roof. Rafe simply grinned with pride and said, "I'm looking for a pony for her."

Rhianna shook her head. "She can't even sit up yet."

"But she likes horses." Rafe pointed his thumb into the stall. "See how she watches that pinto?"

"She'll watch anything that moves," Rhianna argued, unwilling to admit that her daughter already seemed to have an affinity for horses.

The two couples strolled past the stalls where Rafe kept his one-year-olds, the first horses that he'd bred to build the Suttons' reputation. A sleek black foal with an intelligent light in his eyes and long shapely legs tossed his head.

Hal stopped and rested one booted foot on the rail to watch the black frolic. "I like the looks of him. What do you think, Janet?"

Rhianna looked from Rafe to Hal, puzzled. The men were talking as if Hal wanted to make a pur-

PLAY "LUCKY 7" AND GET
THREE FREE GIFTS!

HOW TO PLAY:

1. With a coin, carefully scratch off the silver box at the right. Then check the claim chart to see what we have for you — **2 FREE BOOKS** and a gift — **ALL YOURS! ALL FREE!**

2. Send back this card and you'll receive two brand-new Harlequin Intrigue® novels. These books have a cover price of $4.25 each in the U.S. and $4.99 each in Canada, but they are yours to keep absolutely free.

3. There's no catch. You're under no obligation to buy anything. We charge nothing — ZERO — for your first shipment. And you don't have to make any minimum number of purchases — not even one!

4. The fact is thousands of readers enjoy receiving their books by mail from the Harlequin Reader Service®. They enjoy the convenience of home delivery…they like getting the best new novels at discount prices, BEFORE they're available in stores…and they love their *Heart to Heart* newsletter featuring author news, horoscopes, recipes, book reviews and much more!

5. We hope that after receiving your free books you'll want to remain a subscriber. But the choice is yours — to continue or cancel, any time at all! So why not take us up on our invitation, with no risk of any kind. You'll be glad you did!

YOURS FREE!

PLAY LUCKY 7 FOR THIS EXCITING FREE GIFT!

THIS SURPRISE MYSTERY GIFT COULD BE YOURS FREE WHEN YOU PLAY LUCKY 7!

Visit us online at
www.eHarlequin.com

chase. Yet she knew Rafe didn't plan to sell any of his foals. Why wasn't Rafe asking Hal and Janet who might have kidnapped and left her in their guest cabin? What was going on?

"I think we need a baby like Allison," Janet responded to her husband, without looking at the foal. She cooed in Allison's ear, and the baby waved her hands at Janet's blond hair, seemingly fascinated.

"Come on, Janet. Look at the black. You're a great judge of horseflesh." Hal turned to Rafe with a grin. "Shame on you. You called Rhianna and the baby out here to distract my wife, didn't you?"

Rafe looked pleased. "Yeah. Allison's my secret weapon. With her deep red hair, she's bound to be a beauty like her mother."

Rhianna heated at Rafe's compliment, but she couldn't help wondering if he was trying to distract her from the business at hand. "Are you selling the black?"

"If Hal wants to buy," Rafe said, holding her eyes with a look that pleaded with her not to argue.

All of a sudden Rafe's reason for selling his precious foal hit her like a slap in the face. Selling the art and the cattle must mean that they hadn't raised enough cash to pay back the loan. He needed the money!

Accustomed to thinking of Rafe as rich, she hadn't realized that due to the huge mortgage on the ranch, he might have to raise money to meet the mortgage. His having to sell the horse was her fault.

She knew how much the stable meant to him. This magnificent black was the result of careful breeding and hours of work. Yet Rafe stood there nonchalantly, dickering over a price as if the sale meant nothing to him other than a business transaction.

Rhianna's throat clogged with tears. The reality suddenly sank in. The loan payments must be gigantic. From her window, she'd seen the extra hands come looking for work in anticipation of a giant roundup. Cattle and horses would be sold in hopes the land payments could be made. Because Rafe had paid the ransom, the entire Sutton family would have to turn hard-earned assets into cash.

After Rafe completed the deal and the Stones had departed, Rhianna walked with Rafe back to the house. As if sensing her sadness, Rafe slung an arm over her shoulders. "It's okay. I was going to sell the horse anyway. It just happened a year earlier than I'd planned."

"I'm sorry."

"It's not your fault."

"But—"

"We're going to be just fine. Hal may come back and buy a filly or two."

Rhianna sighed at Rafe's gallantry. "The Stones are profiting from our problems."

"That's just business."

"Is it?" Rhianna wondered, feeling sick at heart. If Rafe had to sell his horses to make the payments, it was only fair that the McClouds help out. But at the idea of selling Sweetness, she barely held back tears.

Still, she vowed to speak with her father soon.

Chapter Eight

Allison Joanne Sutton was six weeks old now, and the first monthly payment to Judge Stuart had been made with the proceeds from the sale of Rafe's foal. Rafe had thought he would mind losing the foal more than he did, but his thoughts tended to dwell on his new daughter and the woman living with him, instead.

Rhianna's cheeks glowed with vitality, and her eyes sparkled with love every time she looked at their daughter. Before he could shut down the thought, Rafe found himself wishing Rhianna would look at him like that. He wondered if she'd ever relax from the exceedingly polite mode with which they treated each other recently—like courteous strangers instead of one-time lovers. He hadn't yet dared to change the conversation from small talk to other matters, fearing they would argue, that Rhianna would take the baby and leave.

Ever since Duncan Phillips had made his despicable offer, Rafe had known that he wouldn't willingly let Rhianna go. But when she'd seemed content to stay with him, he'd simply enjoyed her presence, unwilling to rock the boat.

Around his family, Rhianna was open, but with him she chose her words more carefully. She'd reined in her spontaneous reactions, lassoed her temper and withdrawn her spirited nature.

Despite her air of reserve, she seemed to have fully recovered from the ordeal of childbirth. Rafe wished he could say the same. Seeing his daughter's birth had branded him in inexplicable ways. Ways he neither understood nor liked.

Time and again, he found himself thinking of Rhianna, Allison and himself as a family unit. The bonding that had begun the night he and Rhianna had conceived Allison had strengthened with the time they'd spent together. Allison's birth cemented that bond in every way but one. Rafe had yet to make the connection legal.

As Rhianna walked beside him, the baby strapped to her chest, he warned himself that relationships weren't static. They either dissolved or fused, and if he kept on the path he now walked, he could lose Rhianna and Allison. Right this moment, he should reach out, take both of his women into his arms and tell them how he felt. But he never seemed to have the words to describe the emotions roiling inside him. He kept thinking the churning would stop and he would develop a clear fix on things. But it never happened.

He sensed Rhianna waiting for him to set his hat on straight. But making plans that included a family frightened Rafe on a level he couldn't identify. In fact, he'd never really tried. He'd always known he would remain a bachelor. He wasn't *afraid* of commitment, he'd just never contemplated having a family. While the thought of sharing his life with Rhianna and Allison gave him pleasure, he was happy with his life as it was.

Although Rhianna seemed content right now, he knew without doubt she wouldn't be for long. Once the danger was over, she'd leave with Allison, whether he liked it or not.

And yet he couldn't settle on a path that would take him forward. He couldn't move past the here and now to get to there and then. And he didn't know why. He just knew every time he thought about making any permanent plans with Rhianna, a coldness burned in his chest and his mouth turned so dry he couldn't swallow.

But some secrets he'd kept from Rhianna long enough. He just didn't know how to start sharing them. He'd saddled the horses and asked the senator's cook to pack them a picnic basket. Maybe once they rode out across the land, the constrictions between head and heart would ease.

Rhianna seemed to sense he had a lot on his mind, giving him several thoughtful glances but not asking any questions. He cupped his hands to boost her up, and she swung into the saddle with effortless grace. Allison, thumb in her mouth, looked around, secure in the pack Rhianna wore against her chest.

"Stirrups okay?"

Rhianna tested the length and nodded. "It's good to be on a horse again."

Rafe removed a camera from his pocket and snapped a picture of mother and daughter. This winter during a slack time, he would pull out the photographs and try to make sketches. "I want to record Allison's first horseback ride."

"Along with her first bath, her first smile—"

"You said that smile was gas."

Rhianna tossed a lock of auburn hair over her shoulder, a brief smile on her lips. "I might have been wrong."

As they rode out of the barn into sunlight, Rhianna's hair changed from dark auburn to a fiery red. She adjusted Allison's hat to protect the baby's eyes from the glare, but tipped up her own face to drink in the sunshine.

"I haven't been outside enough."

Rafe could let her talk about the glorious spring weather, a nice safe subject, or he could ease the conversation toward where he needed it to go. After they'd ridden a few miles through green pastures filled with grazing cattle, he still couldn't think of a way to "ease" into the subject, yet feared blurting out his news would destroy any trust she'd started to feel.

Rhianna glanced at him sideways. "Well?"

"Well what?"

"Something's eating at you. You going to spit it out or let it poison you?"

"Are you a mind reader?"

"Stop procrastinating and get to the point," she insisted. She braced her shoulders and tipped up her chin. "There's been no sign of trouble for weeks. If you're anxious to be rid of us, it's probably safe for us to return to Denver. You want Allison and me to pack?"

He shook his head, wondering how he could have

left her feeling unwelcome. "I'm just afraid you *will* leave me after you hear what I need to tell you."

"You want us to stay?"

"Of course." He frowned, wondering where she'd gotten the idea he didn't want her around. Maybe she hadn't been the only one acting distant.

"Are you going to tell me, or do I have to ask Cam to beat it out of you?" she teased.

"He would, too. Cam doesn't like deceptions."

"Neither do I." Rhianna glanced at him curiously. "Just tell me already."

"You won't like it."

She shrugged. "Life isn't perfect."

"Remember the day I came to Denver?" he began hesitantly, figuring that to start at the beginning would be best.

Her glance went to Allison. "How could I forget?"

"After we made love and I left…"

"And you didn't call me…" she prompted.

"It was because we were so good together," Rafe confessed finally.

She nodded and remained silent a moment, as if digesting what he'd just admitted, before drawing her mount to a halt. "You didn't want to get involved."

It was more than that, but he avoided her sharp gaze, dismounting on a rock outcropping, then helping her do the same. "I was determined to forget you."

She and the baby swung into his arms. "It wasn't easy?"

This time there was no avoiding the searching curiosity in her gaze. "It was impossible."

"But you didn't call or visit."

"I thought, eventually, I could get you out of my mind."

She cocked one delicately arched eyebrow. "Really?"

He plunged on boldly. "And then eight and a half months later Daniel called."

"Then you came to Denver to help me. I already know this, Rafe." She eyed him with a frown.

"What you don't know is that Daniel offered to sell me Sweetness if I agreed to help you."

"What!"

He knew Sweetness was her family's hope for prosperity and financial freedom. The McCloud dream to start their own stable rested on that magnificent foal's broad shoulders, in his elegant legs, in his proud carriage. Rafe's agreement with Daniel would have taken the time Sweetness needed to grow and train and race, the time it would take to turn him into a champion.

"I didn't accept his offer," Rafe told her.

"But?" she prodded, folding her arms around the baby as if she already thought the child needed protection from him.

"Your father still believes I agreed to buy Sweetness."

Her jaw dropped as she stared at Rafe, confusion and anger clouding her stormy eyes. "And why does my father think that? Maybe because it's true?"

"He looked at the arrangement as a business deal," he said softly, knowing he was hurting her and wishing he could have avoided it. "And he has his pride. He didn't want to ask for help without offering repayment!"

Sensing the tension between the adults, Allison started to cry. Rafe reached for the baby, and Rhianna jerked back.

"Please, just leave us alone."

"Daniel wouldn't tell me how I could help you unless I misled him," he told her, already suspecting how lame his excuse would sound to her.

"Do you have any idea what that foal means to my father?" She didn't pause to give him a chance to answer. "All his life he's worked for wealthy breeders, sometimes rising at three in the morning to doctor their sick animals, training them through freezing winters. Often the horses' stables were warmer than our own home. Then I won the mare on the rodeo circuit. I thought we should sell her, but Dad insisted we keep her and save for a stud fee. It was sheer luck she went into heat that day at Duncan Phillips's barn. My family could never have afforded Duncan's stud fee, but we aren't thieves. We may not be wealthy, but we don't steal. And we don't take from our friends when they are down."

Rafe had heard enough. He wasn't proud of misleading her father, but he wasn't about to take all the blame, either. "Rhianna, listen to me. I'm guilty of a lot of things, but I don't kick my friends when they are down. In my mind, the deal was off the moment I learned you were in real trouble."

"So you say."

"The horse never mattered. You were carrying my child. I owed you."

"So you helped me out of obligation and duty?"

Why did she make his motives sound so cold? "At

first, yes.'' He ran a hand through his hair. ''Yeah, at first, I'd say I felt I owed you.''

''Well, paying off the kidnapper cleared your debt to me. You and Dad can figure out what to do about Sweetness. You needn't feel guilty, Rafe. I'll get over my hurt. I forgive you.''

He had to give Rhianna credit, she might be upset, but she could see both sides. And he loved her for it. ''When your father came to visit here after Allison's birth, we made an arrangement.''

''He never said a word.''

''I asked him to let me tell you myself.''

''And what is the *new* deal?''

''We're now partners on Sweetness.''

''Really?''

''Your dad thought it only fair that since we mortgaged the ranch to pay the ransom, that he'd give us a partnership in Sweetness in return. Your parents are moving to Highview. We'll stable Sweetness here. We'll train him together. Race him together.''

Rhianna looked at him, her face pale, her lips colorless. ''That's great, Rafe. Everything worked out just fine.''

He would have thought she'd be pleased about the new arrangement. He must have missed something, said something wrong. But what?

She walked away from him toward the grazing horses, leaving their food untouched. He glimpsed a tear glistening on one of her cheeks, and she angrily brushed it aside. She didn't break into sobs, but hugged Allison, rocking her, standing straight and tall and staring at the horizon.

He followed her. "Rhianna, look. Maybe I didn't explain things right."

"You were honest. I'm not angry about Sweetness. You explained very clearly."

Something sure as hell wasn't clear. He had no idea why she'd turned so cold. He had no idea why she'd let loose that single tear. "Sharing Sweetness will remove the financial strain from your family."

"It will," she agreed.

"And when Sweetness wins the Derby, even half the winnings will be enough for Daniel to..." He paused when her features remained expressionless, except for her eyes, which could have been shards of green ice. "It's not Sweetness that has you all lathered up and pulling at the bit like a runaway horse. What's wrong?"

"This is the first chance we've had to really talk since Allison's birth. I just wondered if you're planning to share her with me like we're sharing the horse?"

"We'll work something out."

Her eyes blazed with anger. "Like we worked out Allison's last name on the birth certificate?"

So that's what was eating at her. No longer buffaloed by her behavior, he hesitated to say more and make things worse. "Allison is my daughter."

"You had no right to give her your name without discussing it with me first."

If Rhianna had been remote before, she'd turned into a glacier now. And he had no idea how to bridge the distance she'd placed between them.

She seemed to take comfort in fussing over the baby, changing Allison's diaper, rocking her, singing her a lullaby, ignoring him almost completely. They hadn't exchanged two dozen words since they'd started back toward his house, the afternoon a disaster.

When Rafe heard several cows mooing, he was almost relieved to leave Rhianna and the baby to check. Sometimes cattle got trapped in a steep ravine or stepped in a hole, broke a leg and had to be put down. But he arrived to discover the cows simply appeared nervous.

Rafe couldn't find a reason for the cows' unsettled behavior, and returned to Rhianna, his senses on full alert. Over the years he'd learned that cattle could spook at nothing more than a cricket cheeping, but sometimes they sensed things humans couldn't. "Keep your eyes open."

"What's wrong now?" Her voice might be a tad weary, but one arm curled protectively around Allison.

"I'm not sure."

Out of the corner of his eye, Rafe spotted a glint of glass, an object that didn't belong in the next copse of trees. Further observation revealed a dark outline too regular to be natural, but the figure hid in the shadows, so he couldn't make out if it was a man or another cow. But cows didn't normally have shiny bits of glass that caught the light, and Rafe frowned with suspicion. "Wait here."

He dug his heels into his mount, urged the horse into a gallop, trying to reach the copse of trees before the individual could escape. As Rafe approached, a man lowered his binoculars, doing nothing to hide the fact that he'd been spying on them. Dressed in jeans, a long-sleeved shirt and a battered hat, the stranger didn't seem too surprised that Rafe had spotted him. He simply waited for him to dismount, then tipped his hat in greeting.

Rafe thought he knew all the regular Sutton hands, but this cowboy could have been hired on for the big roundup Tyler had planned. Rafe dismounted and approached, his hand outstretched. "I don't believe we've met."

"I'm Dagny Bitmeyer, sir." The cowboy shook his hand, and Rafe noted a lack of calluses on the palm.

Rafe looked Dagny straight in the eye. "Were you spying on us?"

Dagny couldn't hold his glance. "No, sir. I'm out here to bring in stray cattle."

Suspecting the hand of lying, Rafe looked around. He didn't see any cattle. Instead he spotted a brand on the man's horse—a brand Rafe recognized as Judge Stuart's.

Although he lived most of the year in Denver, Judge Stuart still ran a small operation directly east of the Sutton spread. It was likely Dagny could have bought his horse from the judge and then hired on with the Suttons, but Rafe thought it odd the man had tried to hide in the trees instead of riding on by with a friendly wave.

Rafe had discounted the judge as a suspect after he'd received a call from the kidnapper while the judge had been in the Sutton home. But the judge could have hired help, like Dagny Bitmeyer.

Thinking hard, Rafe rode back to Rhianna. "We need to pay Judge Stuart a visit."

RHIANNA LOOKED AROUND Judge Stuart's place distractedly. Her thoughts kept returning to her disappointing conversation with Rafe and how he'd decided to put his name on Allison's birth certificate when he'd known her wishes. She'd hoped that over the past few weeks they'd grown closer. When Rafe relaxed with Allison in his arms, he looked the picture of the doting daddy, and she couldn't doubt his love for his child.

He always treated Rhianna with courteous respect, never blaming her for the pregnancy, the kidnapping or the enormous debt his family had taken on to pay the mortgage. Sometimes their glances met and they shared a special moment over Allison's baby noises. But then, as if remembering himself, Rafe withdrew.

He didn't go out at night. No other women called the house. He seemed to live like a monk. And the sexual tension that had once simmered between them had disappeared—to be replaced by emptiness. Rafe never touched Rhianna, never cuddled or stole a kiss. His hands-off approach grated on her nerves. But she had too much pride to throw herself at him.

But spending all that time together had been like being a child with no money in one's pockets, looking into a candy shop window and craving chocolate. Just because Rafe had withdrawn didn't mean she didn't ache to run her fingers through his dark hair, smooth away the frown lines on his handsome forehead, kiss him senseless.

Even after their argument over Allison's last name, Rhianna could never stay angry with him for long. She simply liked him too much.

However, Rhianna wouldn't make the same mistake twice. If Rafe wanted to claim her and Allison, he would have to say so—not just put his name on a birth certificate. Rhianna needed to hear the right words. All the kindness in the world just didn't cut it.

So she welcomed the distraction of this trip to Judge Stuart's ranch, while Rafe's sister-in-law watched Allison. As Rafe pulled through the massive stone gates, Rhianna noted the manicured front lawn, the three-story columns and the wide front porch that reminded her of a massive government building, not a home.

Rhianna took in the marble fountain, the solitary statue overlooking the sculpted shrubbery and the ornate ironwork gilding the terrace. "This looks like it could be the governor's mansion."

"Years ago the judge ran for governor against my father and lost. He joked that he might not have won the election but he lived in more sumptuous quarters."

Rafe drove under the covered drive to park, and a uniformed butler opened the front door. "The judge will see you in the library."

Rhianna expected the library to have books, but unlike the floor-to-ceiling shelves of books at the senator's, the walls sported huge windows that looked out onto elaborate gardens. Instead of a warm rug, the floor had cold tile; the wallpaper—gunmetal gray—sported contemporary art.

"Come in." Judge Stuart sat beside a potbellied stove, but stood as they entered. "Can I offer you something to drink?"

Rafe shook the judge's hand. "No thanks. We can't stay long."

The judge peered at Rhianna. "I trust you and the baby have recovered from the kidnapping?"

Rhianna spoke softly. "We're fine, thanks."

"That was a terrible thing. You wouldn't believe the hard-core elements I deal with every day. The criminals are getting younger, the crimes more violent. I'm glad you're safe and sound."

Rafe stood with his hands behind his back, his fingers laced together. Rhianna took a seat by the fire, and the judge did the same.

"So to what do I owe this visit? Have you brought me next month's payment early?"

"You'll get that the day it's due." Rafe spun on his heel in front of the judge and faced him. "You know a man that goes by the name Dagny Bitmeyer?"

The judge folded his hands in his lap. "Maybe I do. Why?"

"He's riding a horse with your brand. My brother hired him for the spring roundup."

"So?"

"I caught him spying on us this afternoon."

The judge narrowed his eyes. "Spying? Don't you think that's a little strong?"

"Dagny's working for you?" Rhianna asked, wondering if this incident had anything at all to do with her stalker. Or was she seeing connections where none existed?

"I thought it prudent to watch my investment," the judge admitted without the least bit of regret.

Had Dagny really been looking for cattle? Watching the Sutton operation for the judge while remaining on the Sutton payroll? Or had he been spying on Rafe and Rhianna?

Rafe found either choice despicable. "You don't think we'll make your payments?"

"I need that money for my reelection campaign. If I'd invested in the market, I'd check with my broker every day. If I'd invested in an apartment building, I'd make sure my tenants stayed employed. It makes sense to keep an eye on the roundup at the Sutton ranch. You miss a payment and I'll be forced to start foreclosure proceedings."

"Nothing in the papers we signed gives you the right to hire our employees to report to you."

The judge threw his hands in the air as if he were the innocent party. "If you're uncomfortable with my business practices, you're free to pay off the balance of the mortgage, and we'll go our separate ways."

Rafe crossed his arms over his chest. "Dad told me you once offered to buy the Sutton ranch."

"I did." Judge Stuart shrugged. "I've made offers on almost every large ranch in the Highview area over the last twenty years. What of it?"

"You ever make an offer at the Stone place?" Rafe asked.

"He won't sell. He says Janet would divorce him if he sold her daddy's place."

Rhianna noticed that the judge didn't really answer Rafe's question, but it was clear he'd spoken to Hal about it, maybe visited the property and knew about the cabin. She also wondered if the judge could have arranged her kidnapping, then lent the Suttons the money to pay the ransom, hoping they couldn't make the payments and that he could foreclose on the Sutton ranch. He certainly dealt with enough criminals in court to help him carry out any nasty scheme he dreamed up.

Could the wily judge have planned and carried out such a diabolical scheme?

Chapter Nine

Rafe and Rhianna shared another ride, this one more pleasant than the last. While Rhianna hadn't mentioned the birth certificate again, he still felt guilty over it. But how could he not claim his daughter? With Allison's future still unsettled between them, Rafe had tried to make their time on his ranch as pleasant as possible, but he sensed Rhianna's patience with him was waning.

He had yet to dismount when one of the hands brought him a message. Rafe swung out of the saddle, helped Rhianna and the sleeping baby down from her horse, then unfolded the note.

"What is it?" Rhianna asked, her eyes a worried green.

"Karen, Judge Stuart's ex-wife, called."

"And?"

Rafe no longer considered keeping information from Rhianna. She had just as much right to know what was going on as he did. "I'm supposed to call her back."

They walked to the house and put Allison in her

crib, then Rafe returned the phone call, putting Karen on the speakerphone so Rhianna could listen in.

Karen spoke so quietly Rafe turned up the volume to hear her. "Remember when you asked me if any of my jewelry boxes were missing?" she asked.

"Yes?" Was one of them gone? Rafe's heart pounded. Just recently, he'd begun to think Judge Stuart could be behind their troubles, but he couldn't be sure when Duncan Phillips also made such a good suspect.

Still, Judge Stuart had been at the party and seen Rafe's interest in Rhianna the night they'd conceived Allison. The judge could have guessed that Allison was Rafe's daughter, and stalked Rhianna until she'd been forced to call Rafe for help. Once Rafe had learned the baby was his, Stuart could have arranged the kidnapping, the mortgage—but what was his ultimate goal? To foreclose on the Sutton ranch? The Suttons fully intended to make the payments. But if Rhianna's stalker had sent those ashes in the Biddle and Baines jewelry box, it might be critical information that Stuart could have had one.

"I'm not sure it's relevant," Karen whispered. "But one of my jewelry boxes has been switched."

"Switched?" Rafe didn't understand. He looked at Rhianna and she shook her head, indicating she didn't understand, either. But she leaned forward, even putting her hand on Rafe's shoulder to steady herself and listen. It was the first time Rhianna had voluntarily touched him since he'd confessed to the bargain he had made with her father. Perhaps she'd eventually forgive him.

"I went to the bank and inventoried my jewelry.

Every ring had a box, but one of them was in an older box, instead of the newer ones the store switched to last year.''

"You're sure?"

"Very. I kept meticulous track of every piece of jewelry. It was the only thing in my name. It was my running-away money. The judge never really wanted me to have it. But he had to show off his wealth. And men like him are expected to buy their wives expensive—''

"I understand," Rafe said with a frown as another thought occurred to him. "When did the judge last have access to your vault?"

"He never did. The box must have been switched when I wore the ring.''

"Can you remember when that was?''

"I'm sorry, no. I just didn't notice until you asked. Am I helping any?''

"I don't know. But I appreciate the information. Thank you." Rafe hung up the phone, discouraged. Each of their suspects could have sent Rhianna the jewelry box. Duncan Phillips, Rhianna's ex-boyfriend, claimed he'd crushed his box and replaced it with a new one which the jewelry store verified. Janet Stone never saved hers. And now the judge's ex-wife claimed she was missing one ring box.

Judge Stuart could have a motive—if he'd hatched the entire scheme because he wanted the ranch. Rafe thought it more likely that Duncan Phillips wanted Rhianna back and would do whatever it took to force her to come to him. Rafe had yet to figure out a motive for the Stones to have been behind the kidnapping, except for one; because of the money crunch,

Hal and Janet were buying foals that Rafe hadn't wanted to sell.

Rhianna sighed. "I feel as if we're running in circles. I wonder if we'll ever know who kidnapped me."

Rafe ached to take her into his arms and reassure her with a hug, but he sensed she wouldn't accept comfort from him. Instead, he ran his fingers through his hair. "Dad would have let me know if the FBI had come up with anything. However, keep in mind that the kidnappers got what they wanted—the money. You and Allison should be safe now."

Rhianna rubbed her hands up and down her arms. "Then why don't I feel safe? Why do I feel as if I'm being watched?"

Rafe risked taking her hand, and led her to the sofa. She didn't sit, but walked to the window. She stared out for a long time, saying nothing. The set of her shoulders, the tilt of her chin told him she hadn't given up. Yet.

How much stress would it take before she broke? Rhianna had always been strong, but he knew how much she worried about the baby's safety. Living with danger hanging over her added a stress factor to their lives that never went away. Every time they drove into town, she looked over her shoulder. He wondered if she'd ever again feel safe.

He could think of few ways to make her feel better. Maybe someone else could. "If you want to talk to someone impartial, Highview has a good psychiatrist."

She spun to face him, anger and surprise warring

in her eyes. "You think I'm crazy? Disturbed after what happened?"

"No. Dagny Bitmeyer *was* watching us. It's not unreasonable for you to think there might be another spy." When she still looked at him distrustfully, his heart ached. He closed the distance between them in three long strides. "I just thought you might feel better if you talked with a professional who could help...."

She glared at him and her lips turned into a fierce scowl. "I don't want a professional. I want—"

A knock on the front door stopped her midsentence, freezing her wild outburst. Without another word, Rhianna whirled and fled upstairs. Rafe debated going after her, but the knocks on the front door continued.

Damn!

Rafe yanked open the front door. "What?"

"And hello to you, too." His brother Chase breezed into the room and gave him a knowing look. "You and Rhianna have a fight?"

Rafe let out a long breath and collected himself. "How'd you know?"

"Been there." Chase punched his brother in the shoulder. "I'm a married man, remember?"

Rafe didn't want to talk about his personal problems, and tried to change the subject. "What was so damn urgent you almost broke down the door?"

Chase knew him too well. "What's so damn urgent it has you buzzing like a bee about to sting itself?"

Rafe slumped into a chair. "I don't know."

"Excuse me?"

"Rhianna's mad at me."

"I figured that out myself. The question is why?"

"I don't know."

Chase went to the liquor cabinet, poured a whiskey and handed it to Rafe. "You must have some idea."

"Not a clue." Rafe downed the drink in one burning swallow.

Chase poured himself a drink and sipped. "When was the last time you told Rhianna you loved her?"

"Never," Rafe mumbled.

"Never!" Chase set down his mostly untouched whiskey, his eyes black with shock. "Are you out of your mind? Women need to be told these things. They need to hear the words. Making love isn't enough for them—you've got to tell them. Repeatedly."

Rafe wasn't about to tell his brother he and Rhianna had only made love once. He picked up Chase's glass and drank his whiskey, too, appreciating the fire in his belly, wishing it would warm his soul.

When Rafe didn't answer, Chase shook his head. "Did you hear one word I said?"

"If I told her how I felt...she'd expect me...to marry her."

Chase's jaw set at a steely angle. "And the problem with marriage is?"

"I don't want that." Rafe looked at his brother, feeling like the biggest heel in the world. "And I don't know why."

"Well, you better figure it out, Bro. And you better do it fast. She's too good-looking, has too much spirit to wait around for you to settle whatever's eating at you from the inside. A woman like Rhianna isn't going to hang around fly bait like you forever." Chase waited for Rafe to say something, but when he didn't even respond to the insult, his brother let out a snort. "I came by to tell you that Tyler fired Judge Stuart's spy. But we're shorthanded and could use your help. You still remember how to ride?"

RHIANNA'S TEMPER HAD propelled her to the top of the stairs after her argument with Rafe, but she'd already started to calm before she reached Allison's room. Rafe might be the most pigheaded man alive, but she wasn't helping him overcome his shortsightedness by keeping their relationship as it was. She couldn't reasonably expect Rafe to conclude how happy they would be together when she kept herself apart from him.

Rhianna knew they couldn't continue living in the same house as polite strangers who mostly avoided the topic of their daughter's future. As she picked up Allison and changed her diaper, Rhianna knew she had to break through the walls Rafe had erected around his heart. For her child's sake, for her sake, she had to give Rafe another chance to see that he was dead wrong about keeping to his bachelor ways.

So when Rafe returned to the house, many hours later, she'd had time to prepare her strategy. She knew he'd be tired after his long day, and with a secret smile, she hoped his resistance to her would be down. She could give him another chance to change his mind.

Rhianna listened to Rafe move around downstairs and bided her time, her stomach fluttering with anticipation.

AFTER HIS LONG DAY, Rafe looked forward to soaking in the big, claw-foot bathtub he'd installed in the bathroom off the master bedroom. His day had consisted of riding drag and eating dust from the herd, while fending off first Tyler's and then Cameron's questions about his relationship with Rhianna. To Rafe's annoyance, Chase had told his brothers about their conversation, and Rafe had had to listen to unsolicited advice all day.

Suspecting Rhianna had long since gone to sleep, Rafe wearily trudged upstairs, rubbing muscles he'd abused. Rounding up cattle was hard, dirty work, and he'd never understood what Tyler and Chase saw in dumb, stubborn cows. As far back as he could remember, Rafe had preferred horses. The senator said Rafe's preferences were in his blood, inherited from his mother, who'd been a first-class horsewoman.

Although his mama had died when he was little, Rafe remembered her with a clarity that sometimes haunted his dreams. He recalled her soft hands smoothing back his unruly hair. He recalled her scent; she'd always worn a light fragrance that reminded him of wildflowers in springtime. But most of all he recalled her telling him that he'd grow up as big and strong as his brothers.

He'd grown taller than Tyler and Chase, ending up as tall as Cam. But he sure as hell didn't feel strong. As he threw his hat onto a peg and slipped off his boots by his bedroom door, he caught sight of his face in a mirror. Dust coated his eyelashes and eyebrows and was caked around his lips.

A cool drink of water first. A shower second. Then the bath he'd promised himself.

He fixed himself a large glass of ice water from the minifridge in his bedroom, tossed his clothes into the hamper and stepped into the shower, letting the warm water sluice the dust from his skin. He soaped, shampooed and rinsed, fighting to keep his eyes open. When he stepped out of the shower, he almost skipped his bath, but knew another fifteen-hour day in the saddle tomorrow would be hell if he didn't relax sore muscles.

He ran his bath, shaving as he waited for the water to fill. With a sigh, he slowly, carefully eased himself into the steaming water, his cool drink of water at his side. Tilting his head back, he rested, letting his thoughts roam as he sipped from his glass. As usual when his eyes closed, Rhianna's face filled his vision. They had to talk. But he didn't know what to say.

When she walked into the bathroom, he opened one eye. "If this is a dream, I don't want to wake up."

She wore an emerald wrapper, and from the way the silky material clung to her full breasts, he suspected she had on nothing underneath. Despite his fatigue, he hardened immediately. He did nothing to hide his response. Perhaps if she saw how much he wanted her...

Her lips curled upward. "Most of you looks exhausted."

"I thought you'd gone to sleep."

She shrugged lightly, making herself comfortable on the lip of the tub, and reached for a wet sponge, then lathered it. "I feel guilty that you're all working so hard to pay off the mortgage."

"We round up the cows every year."

"But this year you'll have to sell so many. It'll

take a decade to recover." She traced the sponge over his shoulder.

He let out a hoarse groan. "Tyler and Chase like nothing better than a good challenge. They're like little kids. I haven't seem either of them so happy in years."

"Lean forward and I'll do your back," she instructed, her tone soft and easy.

He wanted to ask her what else she'd do, but didn't dare disturb the intimacy of the moment with a wisecrack. Moments like these were all too rare between them to risk disturbing the closeness. He intended to savor whatever affection she chose to give him, and count himself the luckiest of men.

He drew up his knees and rested his forearms over them while she dipped the sponge into the bath, lathered it with more soap, then started at the base of his neck. She slid the sponge over his shoulders and down his arms.

She didn't speak and he concentrated on her touch. She took her time with the sponge, making slow, lazy circles over his knotted muscles. He ignored his playful urge to draw her into the tub, kiss her senseless until he convinced her she wanted lusty sex. He'd come to respect Rhianna too much to play with her feelings.

She could see clearly that he wanted her. The first move would have to be one of her making—even if it killed him.

As she dipped her hands to his lower back, he let out a hiss of sheer pleasure. "I'm melting."

"Letting the barriers down?" she asked softly, her

question almost rhetorical, but he knew she needed answers from him, deserved answers from him.

"I'm...trying." He took the hand on his shoulder and placed it over his wildly beating heart. "Feel that?"

"Yes."

"That's what you can do to me just by smiling my way or by walking into the same room."

She dipped her head and traced the arc of his neck with her lips. "What else happens?"

"My awareness heightens."

She licked his earlobe. "You mean just seeing me makes you think about danger?"

"No, silly," he whispered huskily. "I notice the way your eyes reflect your mood, forest green when you go deep in thought, sparkling emeralds when you laugh, glinting green ice when your temper's up."

"I don't have a temper," she retorted with a chuckle that made his insides curl with pleasure.

"Good, then you won't mind sharing this bath with me." He could have toppled her onto his lap, but he'd promised himself he'd wait. With her teasing hands and taunting mouth all over his neck and shoulders, however, his patience had reached its limits. Still, he didn't just take her, but waited for her to accept his playful invitation.

She plopped into his lap with a delightful splash that had him shifting quickly before she damaged sensitive areas. Rhianna wriggled in the steamy tub and let out a sigh of happiness. "I always wanted to be a mermaid when I was a little girl."

"You do have a very nice tail." His hands cupped her bottom, and he shot her his most wicked smile.

Wet satin clung to her breasts and he ached to peel it back. Yet he savored the delay of anticipation, instead leaning forward and nuzzling her breast through the material. He inhaled the light lemon scent from her hair and a hint of talcum powder, courtesy of Allison, combining with the slight musky femininity of Rhianna.

She tilted her head back and closed her eyes, allowing him full access to her graceful neck and generous cleavage. With his teeth, he parted her robe, taking his time to trail his lips across sensitive flesh, to nibble and savor the experience.

Exquisite breasts arched to greet him, and he gently nipped a path along her neckline to rosy-hued nipples that perked up at his attentions. Always a vision of loveliness, her breasts had ripened to a fullness he appreciated and ached to explore.

Wait, he told himself. He needed to make sure Rhianna was enjoying herself. And expectations increased the pleasure.

"Keep your eyes closed," he whispered, his voice husky with need.

She quivered in response to his request, keeping her eyes shut, but her lashes fluttered and her chest heaved.

Rafe reached for his glass of water and retrieved an ice cube. As steam rose from the tub, he taunted her heated flesh with icy droplets that melted off the ice chip.

He let a drop tickle her mouth, and her lips parted. Her tongue licked off the droplet. He had to hold back from kissing her, devouring her whole. Instead he di-

rected another icy drop to her neck, watched it trickle downward.

"You have lovely breasts," he murmured. "Full and so responsive. And they ache for my touch, don't they?"

"Yes."

"But they'll have to wait."

She sighed. Her tummy quivered. "I don't like waiting."

"Don't open your eyes. But stand up."

Abandoning the ice cube, he helped her rise to her feet, and peeled off her soaking robe. Gently, he spread her feet wide. Reached for another ice cube. As steam rose off her body in a mist of heat, he traced the ice cube down her forehead, her nose, her lips. She tried to take the cube into her mouth, but he wasn't done with her yet.

"Cold?" he asked, wondering how they could respond to each other so easily on a physical level when words were so difficult to agree on.

"And hot. I want you, Rafe."

"And I want you," he assured her, circling first one breast with the ice, then the other. He explored her navel, her belly, her hips, and traced a path down her legs to where the water lapped at her calves.

Then slowly, he moved the ice to the inside of her knees and thighs, took pleasure in her trembling need. When she finally figured out his final destination for the ice sliver, she didn't close her parted legs, but quivered in anticipation. He decided to surprise her by kissing just the tip of one lovely breast.

"Rafe. I can't take…much more…of this fire and ice."

"Okay." He switched his mouth to her other breast.

"That's not what I meant." Frustration and desire edged her words.

Lord, he could lose himself in her breasts. Perfectly round, perfectly creamy, with perfect nipples that hardened under his tongue. "You taste so good."

A small moan escaped her lips, and although he reluctantly left her breasts, she tempted him in other ways. He knelt between her thighs. Her hands clenched his hair. Her hips bucked.

With his hands on her bottom, he steadied her hips, thinking he'd found paradise with his lips. She smelled like sugar, tasted like honey. If he could have kept her on the brink for hours, he would have. But he sensed her flesh cooling in the night air.

And the heat running through his veins made him eager to have her. In one swift move he stood, lifted her into his arms and stepped from the tub. "Don't peek."

He carried her straight to the shower, where he let warm water sluice over them to chase away any chill. He'd just started to set her onto her feet when she grabbed his shoulders, wrapped her legs around his hips and planted his sex firmly inside her.

"Hey!"

"Was that a complaint?" she chuckled as she wiggled her hips, thoroughly pleased with herself.

How could he complain when she felt as hot as a volcano about to erupt? Luckily, his shower cubicle was small, the rubber matting nonskid. He planted her back against one wall, and she placed the soles of her feet against the one opposite. He gyrated his hips slowly, with restraint, but she was having none of it.

Her mouth found his. Her hips rocked home. And the steamy pressure inside him built. He'd wanted to go slowly. But Rhianna suddenly clutched him with a spasm, taking him to the brink. Over the edge.

As sensation after sensation washed over him, she let loose a lusty scream. Still joined in the aftermath of loving, he breathed in her breath. Held her close enough that their hearts beat as one.

With trembling fingers, he smoothed the hair off her forehead and looked into her eyes. She was watching his face with an intensity that both exhilarated and frightened him.

He exhaled sharply, knowing the shower was no place to answer the questions he saw in her eyes. Rafe gently lowered Rhianna until she stood on her feet. Putting off the inevitable conversation, one he dreaded, he opened a shampoo bottle and poured soap into his hand. For weeks he'd been itching to run his fingers through her magnificent auburn hair, and he wasn't about to miss his chance.

Spent, she leaned against him, allowing him to wash and rinse her hair. Then he lathered soap into his palms and washed her flesh, unwilling to let a sponge touch her when he so badly needed to do that himself. She had wonderfully silky skin, so soft, so unlike his own.

Finally he turned off the water and wrapped her in a queen-size bath sheet of cotton terry cloth, then swaddled her dripping hair in a turban, before quickly draping another towel around his hips. He wanted to lead her to his bed, but knew if he did they'd just make love again.

"Damn!" he exclaimed, suddenly remembering he'd forgotten something important. Stunned at his own stupidity, he figured he deserved to be shot.

She slanted him a curious look. "Did we splash too much water out of the tub?"

"I forgot to use protection," he admitted. This was a first. Rafe was always careful. He never forgot. How could he have been such an idiot with this woman who meant so much to him?

"It's not a problem," she told him softly.

"Of course it's a problem. Last time you got pregnant when we used a condom. This time I just... forgot."

"I took care of it."

"You're on the Pill?"

She shot him an exasperated look. "If you must know, I used a diaphragm."

Relief washed over him and he sank into a chair. At least one of them was sensible. At least one of them had thought ahead.

Suddenly a new realization struck him like blue lightning. She'd planned to come to him, planned to make love. No wonder she hadn't worn a stitch of clothing under that robe.

His jaw dropped in amazement. He didn't know how, but Rhianna kept surprising him. And the more he learned about her, the more fascinating he found her surprises. She was all-woman. Tender and tough. Spicy and sweet. Fire and ice. The contradictions intrigued him and he wondered if he'd ever understand her.

He cleared his throat in the tense silence. "I'm glad you came to me."

"So am I." She sat on his lap and laid her head on his shoulder. "We're good together."

"I'd say more like dynamite. I don't think straight when I'm around you."

She cocked a brow. "Is that so?"

"I never wanted to hurt you, Rhianna."

"I know."

"But I'm not sure I can give you what you deserve." He tipped up her chin. He didn't really know why he was so opposed to marriage, but he had to find out soon. Or he would lose her. "But if you can give me some time, I'll work—"

Her finger came up to his lips and silenced him. "A relationship isn't supposed to be work, Rafe. If you have to try that hard, then maybe we aren't meant to be together."

Rafe heard the pain in her voice and restrained a curse. What the hell was wrong with him? Despite his best intentions, he'd just made everything worse.

Chapter Ten

Rhianna called herself ten times a fool. When would she get it into her thick, stubborn head that Rafe didn't love her? He was kind, caring. A king among men. He doted on Allison. Rhianna had no doubt he would protect them with his life—because that was the kind of man Rafe was.

But he didn't want her as his wife. He'd made that perfectly clear.

Rhianna had to have been an idiot to hope Rafe would change. Right from the start, he'd told her he liked his bachelor lifestyle. And she'd been dumb for thinking that just because she loved him, just because they were great together, just because she'd had his child, he would one day change.

She shouldn't have come to his room dressed in the flimsy robe. She shouldn't have made herself so available. Even now she had to force herself from the comfort of his lap. Bunching muscle after muscle, she slowly regained her feet. She couldn't look at Rafe, couldn't face him.

After taking her with the passion of a lover, he'd just told her that he needed time to work on their relationship. Obviously he didn't feel what she did, and Rhianna wouldn't settle for less.

It was time to pack her things and leave. With a lump in her throat, a grieving heart and a sorrow so cutting it made her ache, she headed for the door, her head up, holding back tears by sheer force of her will. She wouldn't cry. At least not in front of him.

"Rhianna?"

She wouldn't have turned around except that Rafe's voice sounded as if he were suffering torture. She shoved aside her own pain and spun around, sure he needed help.

Only he looked like a hungry tiger on the prowl, determined, graceful and ready to pounce. The towel tucked around his slim hips enhanced his whipcord torso and lean muscles. He stalked over and placed a hand on each of her shoulders. "I won't let you leave like this."

How had he known she was leaving for good? Or did he just think she would head to her room, not leave his ranch? And why did he have to look so handsome after he'd hurt her so badly?

Knowing she couldn't control the tremor in her voice, she didn't say a word. She just stood there and waited for him to speak, her heart unraveling with disappointment.

Rafe didn't hesitate. "I love you."

Great. Now not only was she an idiot, she was delusional, hearing things.

"Did you hear me? I love you." He looked sincere. His eyes blazed black fire and the corner of his mouth turned upward in a cocky grin. "Do you need to hear it again? I love you."

Maybe she wasn't crazy, after all. Not even she could have dreamed up a scenario like this. Shocked, Rhianna felt faint. She really needed air, but didn't want to move in case the dream would fade and she'd return to reality. Had he really said three times that he loved her?

Rafe cupped her chin, his fingers resting on her racing pulse. Gently, he kissed her forehead, her nose, her mouth, then lifted her into his arms.

She rested her head on his shoulder and marveled over the warmth shooting through her from his touch, from the heat in his gaze, from the marvelous feeling of being loved. She wanted to dance, but being in Rafe's arms was better. She wanted to ask him to tell her again—maybe record his words so she could play them back when she doubted.

He laid her on the bed and climbed on beside her. Turning on his side, elbow crooked, he rested his cheek in his palm, hovering over her. "I've loved you for a long time. I've just been fighting myself."

She frowned at his admission, which was both simple and complex. Why couldn't she have a simple, straightforward relationship? "Is loving me so terrible?"

"I hope not."

Rhianna frowned again in confusion. "I don't know what to say."

"I always thought I didn't want to marry."

She should have known there was no true happily ever after. But his telling her that he loved her took any bitterness out of her words. "You still don't want to marry, do you?"

Rafe sighed. "Since I've known you, I can imagine

us having more children. I can imagine us raising a
family, raising hell, raising champion horses.''

"Why do I hear a 'but' coming?"

Rafe grimaced. "But I can't seem to think how to
go from where we are now to there."

"It's simple. We take a blood test. Send out wedding invitations. We hire a minister, or a notary
and—"

"I'm not being clear."

"Duh." She should have reined in her sarcasm, but
Rafe seemed almost as baffled by his behavior as she
was. "I'm sorry. I just don't understand."

"I'm not sure I do, either. I'm just convinced that
the closer we become, the more danger you'll be in."

"What do you mean by danger? You think the kidnapper will threaten us again? Surely he's off somewhere spending the money, not plotting more evil."

"That's the logical assumption," Rafe agreed. "I
know in my head that the threat to you is over...yet
I can't help feeling that..."

"That what?" she prodded. "That I'm still in danger?" Rhianna didn't hesitate to say the words. If his
fear for her safety was what had kept her and Rafe
apart, she could deal with that. She knew his family
had had more than their share of troubles in recent
years. Rafe's brother Brent had been murdered and
Laura had been blamed at first. Chase had tracked
Laura down and together they'd proved her inno-
cence, and the guilty party had received justice. Then
Cameron's first wife had been killed in Boston, but
her murderer had also been caught. It seemed unlikely
that all these problems were connected until Rhianna
remembered families like the Kennedys—rich, influ-

ential families—often seemed to attract larger-than-life troubles.

Rafe had told her he loved her. That admission would keep her happy for a long time. She could wait for Rafe's fears to ease. Now that he'd given her a measure of hope, he was a man well worth waiting for.

"I never meant for you to feel burdened by my presence here," she said.

"I'd feel better if you stayed close by."

His response made her blush with happiness. Rafe cared for her. He loved her. She still couldn't quite believe her good fortune. She need merely have patience and they would make their family a legal one.

She smiled at him. "I'm living in your house, lying in your bed. How much closer do you want me?"

"Let me show you." He tugged the towel loose from between her breasts and she rolled into his arms.

RHIANNA HAD NEVER BEEN more grateful that Allison now slept through the night. Rafe had made love to her repeatedly, and she perked him fresh coffee before the sun came up. He must be exhausted, yet he went out the door after kissing her lips, whistling some tune off-key.

She sent him off to bring in cattle without mentioning her plan. After feeding Allison, she saddled her horse and headed to the chuckwagon. She could see the smoke from the bonfire from miles away and didn't fear getting lost.

Allison enjoyed the early morning ride. And an hour later, as Rhianna rode into the makeshift camp, she could have sworn her daughter perked up at the sound of her daddy's voice, turning her head and looking around curiously.

"The deadline's tight," Rafe was telling Tyler.

"We can…" When Tyler caught sight of Rhianna and the baby, he stopped talking.

Rafe looked around, spotted her and waved her over, a weary smile of welcome flashing from beneath his Stetson hat. Despite dark circles under his eyes, he still looked sexy in dusty leather. "Anything wrong?"

"You said you wanted me closer." The words came easily to her lips, and they shared a smile over Allison's head. "Have any more of that coffee?"

Hand in hand, they strolled past cowboys riding out after a hearty breakfast of coffee, eggs and ham. They'd already been working for several hours, and dust coated their smiles when they saw Allison or tipped their Stetsons in a polite "ma'am" directed at Rhianna.

She loved this time of the day. Just before dawn, the dew-laden grass and the waning stars lent the feeling of promise to the coming hours. The air had a nip to it with the dark night sky about to be pierced with streaks of a red dawn. Out here, life was more simple. A gal could see across the long green divides from horizon to the distant mountains and know she could be content with a baby in her arms and her man by her side.

Rafe happily took Allison from her, while the cook fixed Rhianna a plate of food and handed her a mug of coffee. Rafe led her to a campfire, where Tyler and Chase stood talking. Both brothers greeted Rhianna, but they made silly faces at Allison, who rewarded them with a huge grin. Rafe looked on proudly.

Rhianna took a seat on a blanket and dug into her mound of food. She chewed with pleasure, swallowed and washed it down with coffee thicker than mud—just the way she liked it. The caffeine jolted her memory of the conversation she'd overheard as she rode in. "What deadline?"

"It's nothing to worry about," Tyler told her with a gallant tip of his hat. Then he turned away. "I need to check the south pasture."

Chase squatted by the fire. "I'll be along shortly."

Rafe, Rhianna and Chase remained silent until Tyler rode off. Then Chase turned to Rhianna. "You'll have to excuse our oldest brother. He still thinks women need protection from the harder aspects of life. Laura's taught me that women deal with trouble just fine—as long as we don't hide the bad stuff."

"Laura's taught you well." Rhianna sipped her coffee, liking the easy way Chase explained his view without criticizing Tyler. "So what's up?"

Rafe lay on his back, placed Allison on his chest and looked up at the sky. "The roundup's taking longer than we expected."

"Why?" Rhianna asked.

Chase held his hands out to the fire to warm them from the early morning chill. "The cows are spread out from the eastern border to the west."

"That's a good two-day ride," Rafe added.

Chase kept talking. "Then we have cows that wandered up the pass, and it's so narrow we have to herd them out almost single file."

"And if it takes longer, you have to pay more men?"

"Not only that," Chase told her in an even tone. "This roundup's not going to be done before the next mortgage payment's due."

"I'll sell another foal," Rafe suggested, more exhaustion than worry in his tone.

Poor man, he'd worked from before sunup yesterday until after sundown, then she'd kept him awake all night making love. He deserved a rest, not another full day in the saddle.

Chase shook his head. "No, Rafe, you already sold your two best. You'll have to go into breeding stock to meet the payment."

"What's the alternative?" Rhianna asked, appreciating that Chase had included her in the conversation. "Can you go to the bank?"

Rafe shook his head and Allison tugged on his chin. "Banks want collateral," he said.

"What about a loan on the cattle—not just the land?" she suggested.

"Apparently our loan to value ratio is too high," Rafe told her.

"That means the bank said no." Chase translated the financial term into English for her.

Rafe patted Allison on the back and the baby closed her eyes. "It's like we've maxed out our credit," Rafe said sleepily.

Rhianna thought about Duncan's offer. He'd pay off the debt—but she would have to marry him in return. After Rafe had told her he loved her, after Rafe had spent the night making love to her, she knew she had to find another way.

''We could sell Sweetness,'' she suggested softly. ''Dad would hate to sell him, but it's not fair that you Suttons should lose everything while we keep that horse.''

She expected Rafe to protest. When he didn't, she looked at him, surprised by his silence. Then she saw why he hadn't argued. Rafe's eyes had closed in sleep.

Chase placed his hand on Rhianna's shoulder. ''I thank you for the offer. But selling that horse would be like selling a member of your family. And we do have other options.''

''What options?'' Rhianna asked, hating the grim tone Chase used, indicating how serious the Sutton financial situation had become.

''We just need to hold on for another month until we round up the cattle.''

''Why not sell the cows in smaller lots?''

Rafe let out a gentle snore. Allison slept comfortably on his chest.

Chase covered them both with a blanket. ''Selling in smaller lots would lower the price. We have a few other assets we can sell first.''

''Like what?'' Rhianna asked curiously. ''Or am I sticking my nose where it doesn't belong?''

''Hey, this is family business. You're family,'' Chase assured her in a way that made her feel accepted, although technically she wouldn't be family until she and Rafe married.

''So what else can be sold?''

''Our mother collected art. We've hired an auction house to sell her collection in New York.''

''Oh, Chase. I don't want you to sell off your

mother's prized possessions.'' Rhianna felt terrible that the Suttons would lose their mother's legacy because of her. The woman had died a long time ago and the fact that the Suttons still had the art must mean that they valued it.

"Don't feel badly," Chase told her. "None of us like her pictures. Dad put them in storage in Denver, thinking one of us would want them after we grew up. He keeps offering them to us, but we don't like Rovell's art—not even Cam's wife, Alexa, our art expert."

"Really? You aren't just saying all this to make me feel better?"

"I'd do that if necessary," Chase admitted. "But it's not necessary. We don't like the Rovell pictures, don't want to pay to insure them, and had put them on loan to a museum in the city. I guess we don't have 'taste,' because they've skyrocketed in value. And the auction house has promised a quick sale. All we have to do is send the Rovells to New York and we'll receive a big fat check." Chase looked over at his sleeping brother and his niece. "The senator thinks you and Rafe should take the art to New York. Lately Rafe hasn't been much use around here."

A chuckle softened Chase's words and Rhianna blushed. She had the feeling Rafe's brother knew exactly what Rafe and she had been doing last night to make him so tired today.

"He didn't get any sleep last night," she admitted softly. "Let's let him rest." She tucked the blanket around Rafe, then dusted off her hands. Rhianna knew her way around horses and cows. She might not be a top hand like Chase's wife, Laura, but she could pull a shift. Rhianna looked Chase in the eye. "What can I do to help?"

RAFE AWAKENED TO FIND Allison wriggling on his chest. He cuddled her closer, then realized by the noonday sun that he'd slept away the morning. While he changed Allison's diaper and wondered where Rhianna had gone, his daughter took in the activities around them with wide-eyed wonder.

During roundup, hands collected cattle from the range, sorted, counted and branded. Tyler had hired ranchers and cowboys from miles around to help, and the men rode out in different directions to gather in the longhorns. His brother had divided the men into groups, and each group gathered strays in one area of the range.

Rafe had fallen asleep after breakfast this morning in base camp. He'd slept while the cowboys had taken fresh horses from the remuda, which was kept in a rope corral near the chuckwagon. The cowboys were returning for a hot meal at noon. And this afternoon they'd count the cattle already brought in, and sort according to their markings. Sick or weak animals were removed from the group and doctored. New calves were branded.

But the most important work, choosing the cows for market, would be Tyler's job. Sometimes the cows objected to their separation from the herd. Calves didn't like being apart from their mothers. It took skilled cowhands on cutting horses to rope and brand the calves. They needed to finish the hot, dusty, dangerous work quickly in order to drive the cattle to market.

As Rafe hefted Allison into his arms, he looked for Rhianna. Her long red hair shouldn't be difficult to spot among all the men. He found her talking with Chase and Tyler.

Clearly she'd been enjoying herself. Her face boasted a tan and a smattering of dust; her green eyes were bright with energy. She caught sight of him as soon as he stepped around the cook wagon.

With quick-footed steps that showed off her long, lean legs, she met him with a kiss and reclaimed Allison. "You needed the sleep," she told him before he could say a word.

He half expected Tyler and Chase to rag him about sleeping on the job. But when he turned to his brothers, Tyler's wind-leathered face had creased in a serious frown. "We've run into a problem."

Chase's jaw had set in a stubborn angle that suggested Tyler underestimated their problem. Rafe slung his arm over Rhianna's shoulder and braced himself for bad news. "Are we missing cattle?"

"Don't know yet," Tyler said, his face bland. "But Rhianna rode out to Silver Pass and it was closed."

Over a hundred years ago, Silver Pass had marked the narrow passageway between two mountains that led to a rich mine. The mine had played out long ago, and now the Suttons used the pass to bring down the herd from the high pastures.

"But don't we have several squads up there gathering in cattle?" Rafe asked, confused and wondering if his nap had somehow impaired his thinking abilities.

"The pass may have caved in *after* they rode

through," Chase said with a sigh. "The men may be trapped there with the cattle."

Rafe turned to Rhianna. "Can we clear it?"

She shook her head. "Not anytime soon. The men can ride out but bringing a herd through is another matter. Either you had one mother of a rock slide..."

"Or?" A sick feeling knotted Rafe's stomach. For weeks, it had appeared as if their troubles were over. They'd had no scares, no troubles outside the ordinary one of raising money to meet Judge Stuart's mortgage on the land.

Had their efforts been sabotaged? Or was he simply being paranoid? He told himself that telling Rhianna he loved her couldn't possibly have caused someone to undermine their roundup efforts, yet deep in his soul he didn't believe it. Somehow he'd known for weeks that the closer he let himself and Rhianna become, the more danger it would bring to them all.

Rafe knew his reasons to remain a bachelor had been inconsistent since he'd met Rhianna. At first, he had never even considered the possibility of marriage—then Rhianna and Allison had burst into his life. And he'd begun to question why he'd always assumed he would remain single. He believed marrying Rhianna would put her in danger—but was that just an excuse? Rafe sensed someone wanted harm to come to the Sutton family. Too much had happened over the past few years for him to ignore the facts. His eldest brother had been murdered, and Cam's first wife had been killed, too. Although both crimes had been solved, Rafe couldn't help thinking that his troubles were somehow connected to other Sutton misfortunes. His thoughts might just be an excuse not to marry—but they were there all the same. And this recent misfortune of someone blocking the pass to prevent the roundup, the sale of cattle to pay off the mortgage, raised Rafe's suspicions even higher.

Rhianna shifted Allison to her other arm. "Someone could have blasted the rock. I'm no expert, but I think it'll take some heavy-duty construction equipment at least a week to clear the rubble."

"Just enough time to ensure the cows won't reach market on time." Tyler ran a hand through his dusty hair. "We'll have to sell the cows in smaller lots."

"We might do better with the art," Rafe suggested.

Tyler placed his hat firmly back on his head. "The auction house needs time to advertise the goods. They need to print a catalog, set a date...."

"Maybe the auction house will give you an advance on the sale," Rhianna suggested, "or auction them over the Internet."

Rafe nodded. "It's a thought."

Tyler rubbed his chin, then gave Rafe a decisive look. "It's time you picked up the art in Denver and left for New York."

"We're on our way," Rhianna agreed.

Rafe, Rhianna and the baby rode back to his house. He made use of his cell phone, making arrangements with the museum to crate the art, calling the airlines for reservations and arranging for the art to be shipped. Finally, as they entered his house to pack, he took Rhianna into his arms and kissed her.

"I should be back within a few days."

"*We* should be back."

Rafe battled with his conflicting emotions. He wanted Rhianna to come with him. The thought of sharing a few nights in New York City with her pleased him. He'd enjoy nothing more than taking her to the eastern racetracks, looking at the foals, contemplating his breeding program and discussing the merits of different animals with Rhianna. Yet he felt she'd be safer here on the ranch.

He knew better than to vocalize his thoughts when he had no rational facts to support them. So instead he held Rhianna tighter. ''Isn't Allison too young to travel?''

''She's weaned and Chase said Laura's volunteered to watch her.''

Allison objected to Rafe holding them so tightly. She let out a squeal of protest, and Rafe and Rhianna broke apart. Rhianna wiped a smear of dust from the baby's face. ''She needs a bath.''

''So do you.'' Rafe reached for the baby, stalling, trying to think of a way to make Rhianna change her mind. But the discussion seemed to be over, and he wasn't sure when or how he'd lost the argument.

Rhianna had a way of manipulating him. And he hadn't yet figured out how she did it. But he didn't mind. He only hoped he could protect her.

Rafe and Rhianna packed their clothes within an hour. It took another thirty minutes to pack for Allison. Rhianna didn't bother to hold back tears as she left their daughter with Laura.

Laura seemed to understand. ''We'll take the best care of her, won't we, Keith?''

Rafe's dark-haired nephew, who looked like a miniature Chase, tugged solemnly on Rhianna's hand. ''I'm a good baby-sitter.''

Rafe didn't hurry Rhianna, hoping she'd change

her mind and decide to stay with Allison. But the stubborn woman wiped away her tears and climbed into the car beside him, blowing her nose into a tissue and letting out a sob.

"Look. Why don't you—"

"Don't tell me what to do."

"But if leaving Allison makes you this miserable—"

"Then I'll just have to be miserable, won't I?" she retorted fiercely between sobs.

"But—"

"Don't say another word. I'll be fine once I stop crying. It's just the first time I've left her overnight. But Laura is a wonderful mother and Allison will be well cared for and loved."

Was she trying to convince him? Or herself? Either way, Rafe didn't say another word. Still he drove slowly, feeling as if with every mile they were leaving a safe niche for the unpredictability of the outside world. He couldn't stop the feeling that having Rhianna with him was a mistake, that bringing her off Sutton property would place her in danger.

All the way to the small airport, he kept checking the rearview mirror for a tail. And after they landed in Denver, he once again searched for anything amiss. He saw nothing wrong, spotted no one suspicious. But that didn't mean there wasn't someone out there.

Chapter Eleven

As they drove through Denver, Rhianna couldn't help wondering if leaving the baby with Laura Sutton had been a mistake. While she knew Rafe's sister-in-law would take good care of Allison, Rhianna still suffered from separation anxiety. No one knew a baby better than her mother. Rhianna knew when Allison wanted her dinner, knew when she needed a nap, knew her schedule without having to look at a clock.

Despite her misgivings, she felt obligated to go with Rafe. That his family had to sell his mother's art collection to pay the mortgage saddened her. The Suttons had given up so much for Rhianna, and now their land, their legacy to their children, was at risk. If only the law enforcement officials would find the kidnapper and the ransom money. The marked bills hadn't shown up anywhere.

With a sigh of frustration at the slow workings of the legal system, Rhianna tried to display some interest as Rafe parked at the Denver art museum. The marble-columned building shaded the busy two-lane avenue with its imposing height.

Rafe opened her car door for her, and she suddenly

wondered if, in her casual skirt and black sweater, she was dressed appropriately. The patrons entering and exiting the building looked as if they'd stepped out of a fashion magazine.

"You okay?" Rafe asked as he took her elbow and escorted her up the graceful steps.

"Just wishing we didn't need to sell—"

"Please stop worrying over the art." He squeezed her hand comfortingly. "We were going to donate the collection to the museum and take a charitable tax deduction. None of the work would have ended up hanging on Sutton walls."

She could hear the truth in Rafe's statement, felt how little the art meant to him. She supposed when one grew up surrounded by wealth, one looked at possessions differently. Rhianna's parents didn't have the money to collect art. But her mother had a pair of silver candlesticks that had been Rhianna's great-great-grandmother's. Rhianna wanted to give those candlesticks to Allison one day. She couldn't imagine having to sell them to strangers.

The museum's interior echoed with the whispers of adults and the murmurs of excited school children on a class trip. Rhianna's gaze took in the enormous crystal chandelier that lit the lobby, the stained glass window that shot arcs of light across the floor, and the elegant brass elevator run by a uniformed security guard.

Rafe led her to the right, and they entered a private office. Inside, the curator, a tiny-boned woman with birdlike features, stood and greeted them. "Mr. Sutton, I'm Marie Valencia. Please come in. We've been expecting you."

We? Rhianna didn't see anyone else in the room as Rafe shook the woman's hand and introduced Rhianna.

"We're sorry to withdraw the art collection from the museum on such short notice," Rafe apologized.

"That's why I've invited some of the museum's other patrons." Marie looked at Rafe over her glasses. "Maybe we can work something out."

As Hal and Janet Stone entered the office, Rhianna's hand tightened in Rafe's. His eyes narrowed a little at the couple and she remained silent.

"Hal. Janet." Rafe nodded a curt greeting and turned back to Marie. "We need to make a seven o'clock flight. Has the art been crated?"

Marie gestured for everyone to be seated. "I'm hoping that won't be necessary."

Rafe refused to sit. Instead, he folded his hands over his chest, gritted his teeth and waited.

Rhianna could guess from his expression that he expected bad news. She half expected the woman to tell him there'd been a fire and the art had been damaged. Maybe the museum had insurance, because the Suttons didn't? Or had the curator discovered the paintings were forgeries?

"Your father had hinted to us that he intended to donate your mother's collection to the museum," Marie began. "And while your family has been very generous to our foundation, and your father had every right to change his mind and reclaim the collection, we have had certain expenses…."

"What kind of expenses?" Rafe asked. His patience made Rhianna's respect for him soar. While she sat on pins and needles and would have allowed her temper to reach the flashpoint, Rafe sat still, as if he had all the time in the world.

"Nothing too drastic, I assure you." Marie's hands fluttered like a bird's wings. "Brochures have been published, advertisements sent out. As an added expense, we've decorated the Rovell room to match his works."

Rafe discreetly looked at his watch. Rhianna knew they still needed to see the art crated and loaded on trucks and driven to the airport, and Rafe didn't want to rush the delicate job.

Janet Stone stood and fluffed out her skirt, drawing attention to her shapely legs. Rhianna bit back a smile of satisfaction when Rafe refused to look.

Rhianna was glad Rafe didn't like games. While they were patrons of the museum, the Stones didn't belong here, meddling in his business, and Rhianna wondered if the kidnappers had held her on the Stones' property because it was isolated, or because the Stones knew she wouldn't be found there by accident.

Janet moved to stand behind her husband. "We're sorry for your troubles, Rafe." She smiled too brightly. "We thought we could buy the Rovell collection from you, donate it to the museum, and then none of the works would have to move."

Rafe frowned at Janet and Hal, then hid his suspicion behind a mask of unconcern almost as soon as Rhianna spied it. But Rhianna's brain asked question after question. Why were the Stones so interested in buying what the Suttons had to sell?

Marie fidgeted in her chair. "The sale would benefit the museum and help you sell—"

"I'm afraid it's too late," Rafe said, without waiting to hear the monetary amount of the offer. Rhianna knew he'd never show his annoyance at his neighbors' interference into his affairs, but she was aggravated enough for both of them. "We've already signed a contract consigning the Rovells to a New York auction house."

"Oh, how dreadful." Janet's tone turned overly dramatic, and Hal shook his head as if agreeing with his wife's sentiments.

"You can always bid on the art in New York," Rhianna suggested, making her tone artificially sweet and catching a glimpse of amusement in Rafe's eyes.

Janet fingered one of her five-carat diamond earrings. "But it just seems such a bother to fly all the way to New York and bring the paintings back here."

Hal shrugged. "The boy's signed a contract, Janet. He can't go back on his word."

Rafe nodded and turned back to Marie. "I'm sorry, but we have a plane to catch. Could you take us to the Rovells and have your people start packing the works right away?"

Rhianna thought the Stones would leave, but they trailed after Rafe and Rhianna as Marie led them to the room where his mother's art hung. At least the curator was efficient. She had the room closed to visitors, and the packers arrived within minutes.

Janet took Rhianna aside but did nothing to prevent the men from overhearing her false joviality. "And how's the baby? I'm surprised you could leave her."

Janet's tone didn't have one iota of threat in it, but Rhianna tensed anyway. "Allison's great. And she's well protected on the ranch."

"I guess." Janet leaned close to Rhianna's ear, but her whisper must have carried across the room, because Hal flinched. "I've always wanted a baby, but it's the only thing Hal refuses me."

"I'm sorry," Rhianna said politely, wondering if the woman had a point for making her disclosure.

Rhianna lost track of Janet's patter as she listened to Hal's and Rafe's conversation. Hal stopped in front of a particularly dreary Rovell. "I thought the offer to buy these would help you out."

Rafe kept his composure and his smooth Western manners. "I appreciate the thought."

"You going to make the judge's payment this month? I heard you had trouble at Silver Pass."

Word sure got around fast. Was Hal's interest in Rafe's business just neighborly? His showing up here at the museum had raised Rhianna's suspicions. The Stones were natural busybodies, but until now she'd always figured they were harmless.

She listened for Rafe's response, knowing he didn't believe in confiding in casual acquaintances or business associates. He shared his problems only with family.

Rafe lined up several crates by the back door. "We're going to be fine."

His voice sounded so confident. Rhianna only wished she could be as certain as Rafe sounded.

RAFE AND RHIANNA LANDED at Newark Airport in New Jersey after the flight had been delayed a half hour. While Rhianna called Laura to check on Allison, Rafe arranged for a truck to transport the Rovells to the auction house—which was staying open late just for him. Then he and Rhianna watched the crew unload the crates from the plane and place them onto a truck. They followed the vehicle until it was unloaded, at which point the auction house signed a receipt for the goods.

With the receipt in hand, Rafe appeared to relax, and said he looked forward to checking into a hotel. For her part, Rhianna wanted a hot shower, maybe room service and a romantic evening with Rafe. As he led her through the hotel lobby toward the elevator, he spoke softly in her ear. "Do you realize this is our first night alone together in almost a year?"

Rhianna tossed her hair over her shoulder. "Is Allison cramping your style?"

"I've learned to schedule around her," Rafe admitted without an ounce of complaint entering his tone. His eyes shone with sincerity, while revealing a banked sensuality that tripped her pulse. "But I'm looking forward to having you all to myself."

Rhianna wanted this time with Rafe. They'd had so little romance in their relationship. Everything had been done out of order. She and Rafe had never been on a date. Yet they had a child together. They'd suffered through a crisis together, but were not yet married and had never had a honeymoon. They'd never really had time to explore one another at a less-than-frenetic pace except for that one night in the tub. Tonight she ached to put aside the possibility of the Suttons losing the ranch. She wanted to forget the kidnapper had never been caught. She just wanted to have a romantic evening with the man she loved.

Maybe if he trusted her, really trusted her, he would confide in her and reveal why he still resisted marriage. She believed he loved her. Knew he loved his daughter. And she wanted them to be a family in every way. Rhianna vowed to have patience. Rafe had told her he loved her, and she wouldn't press for more. Not yet. She would give Rafe all the time she could. And she refused to think about what she would do if time ran out.

Nothing was going to spoil this evening. With a smile on her face, Rhianna had tucked in a nightgown of sheer emerald lace, a color that brought out the highlights in her eyes. She couldn't wait to see the look on Rafe's face when she wore it for him.

Rafe opened the door and Rhianna sucked in a gasp. She'd traveled the country with her family, often staying in budget hotels. She'd never seen a room like this, with a cozy fireplace tucked in a corner, a desk with a massive bouquet of fresh flowers, a computer, a fax machine and a spare phone, a king-size bed with a satin coverlet folded back to reveal crisp white sheets.

She twirled around and sat on the bed, bouncing with abandon. "Rafe, can we afford all this?"

"One night won't break us." With a smile at her pleasure, he sat beside her and kicked off his shoes, then lay back with his hands laced behind his head. "Someday we'll come back and spend a week."

That sounded good to Rhianna. Rafe didn't refer to their future together often, so whenever he did, she cherished the moment, locking it away like a keepsake, taking it out to examine when she doubted they had a future together. But now was not the time for deep thinking.

Rhianna scooted next to Rafe and started to unbutton his shirt. The phone rang and her fear thudded through her. ''Allison!''

The baby she'd left with Laura was never far from her thoughts.

Rafe picked up the phone and motioned for Rhianna to listen on the extension. ''Hello?''

She hurried to the desk, telling herself she'd just spoken to Laura less than an hour ago and the baby had been fine then. But babies could come down with fevers quickly.

Get a grip.

Even if Allison had taken sick, Cameron would know what to do. So why did she feel so guilty for leaving Allison?

Rhianna picked up the receiver, prepared to hear Laura speak. But the voice was male. Unfamiliar. ''Mr. Sutton?''

''Yes?''

''This is Mr. McPherson from the Weston Auction House.'' A wave of relief washed over Rhianna and weakened her knees. She sank into the nearest chair as the stranger continued, ''I'm afraid we have a problem.''

Oh, no. Had the art been damaged? Rhianna looked across at Rafe. His expression remained stoic, but she could see a hint of despair in his eyes. Since they hadn't finished the roundup and the cattle remained unsold, they needed to sell the Rovells to meet the ranch's mortgage payment.

''What kind of problem?'' Rafe asked.

Mr. McPherson's voice remained brief and businesslike. ''I'd prefer to discuss this in person. Could we meet at the auction house in an hour?''

"Look, we've spent the day flying from Highview to Denver. Then we crated the art and flew to New York. We're tired. Can't we settle this on the phone?"

"That's up to you, sir. The Rovells aren't here."

Rafe rubbed his forehead. "What do you mean, they aren't there? We saw them unloaded. I have a receipt for them."

It seemed as if Murphy's Law was haunting them—everything that could go wrong would go wrong.

"Have they been stolen?" Rhianna asked, unable to keep the horror from her tone.

"Not from us. We unwrapped crates of framed posters, not original art."

"Posters?" Rafe asked.

"Someone pulled a switch. I suggest you call the police," McPherson suggested. Before he hung up, he gave them a phone number where they could reach him that evening.

Rhianna put down the phone, shocked. Rafe had already grabbed a pad and pen and begun making notes, and she could only marvel at his presence of mind in the face of another disaster.

She came over to him and placed a hand on his shoulder, knowing their romantic evening had been ruined. "What are you doing?"

"Making a list. We saw the Denver museum pack the art. We saw the art placed in the delivery truck. We followed the delivery truck to the airport, where we watched them load the art onto the plane. Then we saw the art come off the plane in New Jersey, and we followed the van to the auction house. So where was the switch made?''

"Maybe at the auction house after it arrived?" Rhianna suggested.

Rafe wrote her idea on his pad. "It's possible, but unlikely. I'm sure their security is tight."

"But that art wasn't out of our sight during the entire trip."

"Sure it was," Rafe argued. "We didn't actually ride in the trucks or the cargo hold of the plane."

"No one could have switched the art during the airplane ride because the cargo hold isn't pressurized."

"Okay, let's concentrate on the two trucks. In Denver, we watched them crate the art and place it inside the truck."

"And then we went to get our car," Rhianna reminded him. "We took what? Maybe two minutes before we caught up to the truck outside."

"Probably more like five minutes. Not long enough to unload the art and reload the fakes."

Rhianna's mind switched from shock into overdrive as adrenaline flooded her. "Suppose someone simply switched the trucks?"

Rafe looked at her in amazement. Then he leaned over and kissed her. "You're brilliant."

She leaned into the kiss, threaded her fingers through his hair, enjoying his appreciation of her suggestion. "Shouldn't we call the police?"

"Yes. And I'm also going to phone Dad and have him start the Denver authorities investigating." Rafe stood and held out his hand to help her to her feet. "Sorry, but we need to fly back tonight."

"I understand."

Regret darkened his eyes. "Taking the red-eye is not how I planned to spend the night."

"There'll be other nights," she promised him, hoping that before they landed back in Denver the missing Rovells would be found.

As soon as the pilot gave permission and they'd landed in Denver, Rafe powered up his cell phone and called the senator. "Any news?"

Rhianna unbuckled her seat belt and stepped into the crowded aisle. His father's voice came through the air waves loud and strong. "The Rovells are still missing, but I think you should pay Duncan Phillips another visit."

"Why Duncan?"

At Rafe's question, Rhianna's brows went up. He leaned toward her and tilted the cell phone so they both could hear his father's answer. "You thought the trucks that transported the art might have pulled off a switch, right? Well, guess who owns the coast-to-coast trucking company?"

"Duncan?" Rafe guessed. Just when he'd been thinking the number one suspect behind his troubles had to be the Stones or Judge Stuart, new suspicions about Duncan arose. Duncan had been at the party the night Rafe and Rhianna had made love. Jealousy could have caused Duncan to stalk Rhianna, with his ultimate goal being to get her back when she needed help. He could have kidnapped Rhianna and forced the Suttons to pay the ransom with one evil purpose in mind—to make Rhianna come back to him when the Suttons couldn't make the mortgage payments.

Duncan Phillips had the means, opportunity and motive to pull off the series of criminal acts. He also had the arrogance to think he could get away with it. Rafe wished Rhianna weren't with him. He ached to confront Duncan alone.

As they exited the airplane, Rhianna bit her lip, a troubled look in her eyes. "I didn't know Duncan owned a trucking company."

Rafe spoke through teeth clenched in anger. "Apparently, there's a lot about the man we don't know."

"Who picked Duncan's trucking company to ship the Rovells?" Rhianna asked.

"Good question." Whenever he thought how poorly Duncan had treated Rhianna, Rafe's blood pressure went up. Thinking that the man might have deliberately stolen the art so the Suttons couldn't make the payments on the land made Rafe furious. Realizing that Duncan could have been the man who'd kidnapped Rhianna and put her and Allison's lives in danger made it impossible for Rafe to concentrate on the facts. But he had to. They had no proof that Duncan had done anything wrong.

Right now, Rhianna's thinking was clearer than Rafe's. At least she wanted to pin down the facts. Rafe took out his cell phone and dialed the Denver museum. The curator wasn't in but her assistant gave him her home phone number.

Marie's sleepy voice answered the telephone. "Yes?"

"This is Rafe Sutton. Sorry to wake you, but we think the Rovells were stolen off the truck. Did you pick the shipping company?"

"Yes. I did. They came highly recommended."

Rafe frowned, wishing he'd gotten more sleep. He had the feeling he was missing something besides their luggage, which had failed to show up at the baggage claim. "Don't you use a standard company?"

"We don't often need to hire an entire truck. You have an exceptionally large collection," Marie told him.

"So who recommended the trucking company?" Rafe asked.

"Hal Stone said they were the best." Marie yawned, but her voice became defensive. "I had no reason to doubt Mr. Stone."

"Thank you for the help, Ms. Valencia."

Rafe took Rhianna's hand and headed for their parked car. "Hal recommended that the museum use Duncan's company."

"Hal's always offering his opinions," Rhianna said. She must have caught the look of speculation in Rafe's eyes. "What? You think Hal and Duncan are in cahoots against us?"

"I don't know." Rafe unlocked the car door. "I'm tired. Hal might not even know that the company he recommended belonged to Duncan."

Rhianna put on her seat belt and rubbed her eyes as Rafe started the car. "Where're we going now?"

"We need to talk to Duncan."

"It's six in the morning."

Rafe pulled into Duncan's home before seven. He didn't care if he disturbed Duncan's sleep. He didn't care if Duncan didn't want to see him. Rafe wanted answers.

Duncan, fully dressed in a suit and tie, answered the front door. "I can't help you."

Rafe walked right into the posh foyer without waiting for an invitation. Rhianna stayed at his side, frowning at Duncan. "You don't seem surprised to see us."

"I figured you'd come to me." Duncan smirked at Rhianna and jerked his thumb at Rafe. "I just didn't expect you to bring him."

"Why not?" Rafe challenged with a lift of one brow that he hoped irritated the man as much as Duncan's attitude grated on him.

Rhianna stepped between the two men. "Duncan, we came because you own a trucking company that transported art—"

"Sutton art," Rafe interrupted.

"—from the Denver museum to the airport," Rhianna explained. "Only the art never arrived at Newark airport. Someone switched the trucks. We got posters and the art vanished in one of your other trucks."

"Can you prove that?" Duncan asked. When Rafe hesitated, Duncan shook his head and folded his arms over his chest. "And you suspect me?"

"We didn't say that." Rhianna glared at Duncan, and Rafe applauded her silently for standing up to the bully.

Duncan practically growled a threat at Rhianna. "You'd better not make accusations you can't back up."

Rafe would have liked nothing more than to plant his fist in the man's sneering face. Instead he decided to hit Duncan where it would hurt more—in his pocket. "I'll expect a check from you to cover our losses this morning."

Duncan shook his head. "My insurance company handles all the claims."

Phillips Insurance. Was there a company in Denver the man didn't own? Rafe took Rhianna's hand, knowing the intimacy would annoy Duncan. "Fine. I'm sure your check will be good."

Duncan rocked back on his heels. "It's not that easy."

"What do you mean?" Rhianna asked.

"My insurance company can't release any funds until the police investigation is over. And you know the law enforcement people are overworked and underpaid. I expect the investigation could take months!" Duncan exclaimed. He was practically gloating.

Rafe didn't let the effect of Duncan's words show on his face. They didn't have months. They had only a few more days to make the next mortgage payment.

Chapter Twelve

Rhianna couldn't believe that she'd let Rafe talk her into breaking and entering the Stones' house. Actually, he'd tried to insist that she stay on the Sutton ranch with Allison, but she'd refused to let him take all the risks alone. His family wouldn't be close to losing the ranch if they hadn't paid her ransom, so she would go with Rafe even if she thought what he intended was dead wrong.

Since the Stones were still in New York, no doubt hoping the art would be found and that they could buy it, Rafe thought today a perfect one to do some snooping. Rhianna looked through the windshield at the mountains and wondered who would take care of Allison if they both were caught and sent to jail. But she didn't voice her worry. Clearly Rafe already had too much on his mind.

A man of contrasts, he drove with the casual demeanor of a Colorado native accustomed to steep roads, sharp switchbacks and loose gravel, yet his eyes burned with steel-gray boldness and quiet determination. His shoulders were relaxed under his denim shirt, but a muscle in his jaw ticked as he whistled a country tune.

Rhianna looked at the wind-whipped trees beneath the low storm clouds and shivered. She knew all about the seductive beauty of the Colorado high country. But she wasn't deceived by the season. Even in summer, the thin air made the chill lodge in her bones. "Are we going to hide the car and hike in?"

Rafe shook his head. "Looks like rain. I'd prefer to drive through the front gate."

"But don't the Stones have a caretaker for the house while they are out of town?"

"I don't think so. They keep a groomsman and exercise boy for the horses at the far end of the property."

Rhianna tried to recall the layout. The last time there, she'd been in labor and distracted by her circumstances. All she could remember was that the cabin had been far enough away from the main house that if she'd shouted for help, no one could have heard her. She'd never seen a barn, but the Stone property was a large one, at least a few thousand acres. They didn't raise cattle on their hilly land, but kept the place as a second or maybe third home, to visit during ski season or during Colorado's glorious summers.

"Suppose someone sees us?" Rhianna asked, though she thought that unlikely with the way the rain streamed down. Anyone with sense would hole up under a dry roof next to a warm fire.

"I'll ask to be let into Hal's study."

"But—then Hal will know we've been here."

"So? I'll simply say my cell phone went dead and we needed to make a call. Will you relax?"

"And if no one sees us?"

The corner of Rafe's mouth turned up. "Then we won't have to explain our presence, will we?"

Rhianna sighed. Rafe seemed to have an answer for everything. He didn't appear uneasy about blatantly driving through the rain to the Stones' home and prying into their personal belongings. He seemed to have nerves of steel.

"What exactly will we be looking for?" Rhianna asked, raising her voice to be heard over the patter of pelting rain. "Surely you don't expect to find the marked ransom money under Hal's desk?"

"Now that would be lucky." Rafe smoothly turned down the private road shaded by tall pine trees. "I'm hoping to find a calendar with notes on it, a diary, maybe a list of phone memos that connect him to the art theft."

Rhianna didn't like the idea of reading the Stones' diaries, and hoped the situation wouldn't come up. Uneasy, she shifted in her seat and, through the foggy window, surveyed the house, a massive A-frame with cedar walls and an acre of glass that reflected the mountainside. No dogs barked. No cars stood in the driveway. The home looked deserted, but as Rafe parked by the front walkway, Rhianna felt as if someone might be watching. Yet no curtains moved, and the only sounds besides the pounding rain were the ones she and Rafe made.

"Now what?"

Rafe raised an eyebrow. "We knock on the front door."

Rhianna tried to calm her racing pulse but it did absolutely no good. Her stomach knotted and twisted, and she was glad she'd skipped breakfast this morning. She wouldn't make a good thief and was sure that her trepidation showed on her face. Rafe didn't seem to notice.

They ran up the front steps and arrived only half-soaked. Rafe rang the doorbell. A pleasant musical chime sounded. They waited. Shivering, water droplets running down her neck, Rhianna shifted from foot to foot, unsure whether or not she hoped someone would open the door.

"Looks like no one's home."

Rhianna nodded, her mouth too dry to speak.

When Rafe reached into his pocket, pulled out a key and inserted it into the lock, her jaw dropped in amazement. "Where did you—"

"Hal gave it to me." Rafe shot her a cocky grin, and she wanted to hit him for making her think they were going to have to break in through a window.

"W-why did he give it to you? When?" She almost stuttered in her relief. If Hal had given Rafe a key, no one could arrest them. Their being here was legal.

His grin warmed her. "After your kidnapping, when Hal and Janet bought my first foal, I mentioned the FBI might need access to the property again to search for clues in the guest apartment. Hal gave me a set of keys and asked me to lock up when the law enforcement officers had finished."

"That doesn't sound like the action of a guilty man," Rhianna commented, wondering why she still couldn't settle the nerves in her stomach.

Rafe opened the door and then led her inside. "Hal is one of the most brilliant men I've met. However, I never understood what he sees in Janet."

"Why? She seems harmless." Rhianna walked over the slate-covered floor of the foyer and stared at the magnificent nude painting of Janet Stone that hung in the front hallway.

"Hal had her painted on their honeymoon."

In the painting, Janet stood with her fists planted on her hips, a secretive smile on her face, her long blond hair blowing in the wind. Her skin glowed with a radiance that gave her an almost angelic appearance. "She's gorgeous."

Rafe ignored the nude. "She's an airhead. I've never understood how a man with Hal's intelligence could remain interested in her all these years."

"Maybe he's interested in her…other attributes."

"I guess." Rafe wandered to the left hallway, and Rhianna followed, somehow pleased by the conversation. Right now, she was an attractive woman. But beauty wasn't what she wished to base a relationship on. She'd always known Rafe valued her opinion, and it was nice to know physical beauty wasn't high on his list of priorities. She'd never wanted to be one of those woman who had to diet or color her hair or have a weekly pedicure to keep her man's attentions. And Rafe seemed content with their relationship—maybe too content. He sure didn't seem in a hurry to set a wedding date.

As the storm outside subsided, Rhianna told herself that she'd promised to be patient. But waiting was so difficult. With all the uncertainty around them, she wanted to know that whatever happened, she, Rafe and Allison would be together as a family.

Rafe led her into a dim office. She expected him to flip on the lights, but instead he drew back drapes to reveal a spectacular view of a mountain waterfall. Despite the rain, deer gathered around a salt lick and birds flitted from branch to branch among the huge evergreens that clung to the rocky riverbank.

Rhianna stared out the window. "Wow!"

Rafe thumbed through papers on the big desk, while Rhianna turned from the window and wandered about the room, reluctant to touch anything. Oil paintings hung on the wall, some with signatures that even she recognized. "I'm surprised the Stones don't have a burglar alarm."

"Those are copies," Rafe told her. "Not even Hal can afford the originals."

She wandered past a bar made of cherry and smoked mirrors to a smaller desk. Janet's? Hal and Janet's framed wedding picture rested next to an elegant crystal bottle of perfume, a purple feathered pen and personalized lavender stationery. Tucked neatly on the corner of the desk was a list of stocks, buy and sell orders, dated on the same line.

"Rafe?"

"Umm?"

"Is this Janet's desk?"

"Probably. She likes to putter while Hal works."

"Well, she was doing a lot more than puttering. These buy and sell orders are for millions of dollars in stock."

Rafe didn't look up from his investigation of a boxful of papers. "Janet had no interest in cattle."

"Not that kind of stock. I'm talking Dow Jones Industrials and mutual funds."

"Janet? Who would have thought she knew about such things? And why does she hide her intelligence?" Rafe approached and frowned at the papers Rhianna handed him. "She bought and sold commodities, too—gold, pork bellies, corn. And she wasn't doing well." He pointed to a notation. "Look at these margin calls. She paid off these debts soon after we paid the ransom."

Rhianna could hear the incredulous note in Rafe's voice. Clearly he had trouble believing that Janet Stone could be so intensely involved in the buying and selling of stocks and commodities. She'd fooled Rhianna, too. As Rhianna looked at the margin calls, she wondered whether Janet had a gambling problem and, if so, whether her husband knew about it. "You think she could have paid the margin calls with the ransom money?"

RAFE CONSIDERED RHIANNA'S question as they drove into Highview. The storm had cleared and left behind a fog and humidity that forced him to turn on the car air-conditioning. "Margin calls are paid by check or bank wire. Janet would have had to launder the cash before she could put the bills in the bank—and Dad says the FBI has found no sign of the marked cash entering into circulation."

Rhianna sat back in the car and closed her eyes. "So now what?"

She'd kept her tone neutral, but Rafe knew how badly she wanted to go home, take Allison in her arms and relax for a few hours. He wished he could give her the time she yearned for. But if they didn't figure out within the next twenty-four hours who had kidnapped Rhianna and taken the ransom money, the Suttons would lose the ranch.

Rafe sensed they might be closing in on the culprit. He didn't know why he felt that way, especially when he was no closer to figuring out who his enemy was. But the feeling within him was strong. If he just kept chipping away at the suspects and their stories, the culprit was bound to make a mistake. And Rafe intended to be there when it happened.

But his efforts were taking their toll on Rhianna. He knew she felt guilty over what had happened. No matter what he said, he couldn't seem to lighten her mood. Not even telling her he loved her removed the worry from her eyes. Just as Rafe sensed that they were closing in on the kidnapper, he sensed Rhianna slipping away from him again. She might sit right next to him in the vehicle, accompany him as he questioned and searched, but she'd once again lost her enthusiasm and had become discouraged.

Seeing her hurt made him hurt. But he didn't know what to do. As long as the Suttons owned the land, Rafe would fight to keep it. But the harder he battled, the guiltier Rhianna seemed to feel, and he had no idea how to break the depressing cycle.

"Judge Stuart keeps an office in Highview. I thought we'd do a little exploring."

Rhianna opened her eyes. "I thought the judge lived in Denver."

"He does now. But he grew up in Highview and keeps a small office here. His spread lies just east of our ranch."

"Are he and the senator friends or rivals?" Rhianna asked, and Rafe could see her trying to fix the relationship in her mind. It was what he admired about Rhianna. She wanted the truth. She wouldn't settle for less, and she had a special ability to see below the surface, to delve into the complexities of life.

"I don't know if *friend* is the right word. Highview is a small town. There aren't that many men my father's age who share the same economic status. Powerful men tend to play cards and golf together, run against one another at election time, compete for the same women—"

"Were there other women besides Karen?" Rhianna turned to him with questions in her eyes.

"As far as I know, Karen Stuart was the only one."

"Were there any hard feelings?" Rhianna asked.

Rafe shrugged. "Since the judge got Karen, I don't see how he could have held that against my father."

Rhianna mulled that over while Rafe pulled onto the highway. "The judge could hate your father for defeating him in the senate race."

"Years ago, he also ran against my father for governor and lost. He didn't come unhinged then, so why would he act crazy now? I don't think the political race was especially bitter, and the judge certainly has enough money. I don't think he's our kidnapper."

"Unless money isn't his motive," Rhianna reminded him. "Maybe he wants the ranch."

"There's another possibility, too," Rafe said reluctantly. The gray clouds opened once more and released a pelting rain, and he flipped on his windshield wipers.

"What?"

"Your stalker in Denver may have had nothing to do with the kidnapper," he murmured. "It could have been two completely different people. And the kidnapper might not be someone we know, but a stranger, a professional who took you simply to collect the ransom."

"But you don't think that, do you?" Rhianna pressed, and he realized how well she knew him. Sometimes when he looked into those wide eyes of hers, he would swear she could read his mind. If only she could—then she would see how much he wanted them to have a future together, how much he wanted them to be a real family...how much he wanted to understand and banish his misgivings about marriage.

Fog condensed on the windshield and Rafe turned on the defroster. "My family has had an unusual number of problems in the last few years. Suppose someone behind the scenes is manipulating people to do my family harm?"

Rhianna jerked and her eyes widened even further. "Is that what you think?"

"It's just a possibility...."

"That's why you don't want to get married, isn't it?" She nailed him with the truth, her voice sharp, but understanding dawned in her eyes. "You think that if you marry me something bad will happen?"

"Don't make it sound so far-fetched. My eldest brother was murdered—"

"And his killer caught."

"Cam's first wife was murdered—"

"And I was kidnapped. But I'm not a Sutton. Since we aren't married, your theory makes no sense."

"But you were carrying *my* child. We were connected. And apparently someone figured out that connection."

As she mulled over his theory, her tone reflected her sadness. "It's never going to be over. You're never going to feel that we're safe. It's not fair that someone has taken control of our lives. I hate this helpless feeling. I hate living in dread of the next bad thing."

Rafe pulled the car over onto the shoulder, turned off the engine and drew Rhianna against his chest. "We're going to catch whoever is behind our problems."

Rhianna jerked away from him, fury and melancholy battling in her expression. "And what if we don't solve the problem? What if we never figure out what happened? You aren't going to marry me, are you?"

With every fiber of his being, Rafe wanted to give her the answer she wanted to hear. But he couldn't. How could he marry her when he was irrationally convinced that doing so would put her life in jeopardy?

Rhianna took out a tissue and angrily blew her nose. "I think your theory is a crock of sour milk. Our baby will be talking soon, asking questions. And when she doesn't have married parents, what are you going to tell her?"

"I can't put your life in danger," Rafe told her miserably, fully aware that she expected more from him than he could give. He wrapped his fingers around the steering wheel and tried to think of a way out. Once again, he came up empty.

Rhianna's eyes flashed her anger. "*You* aren't putting my life in danger."

"Really?"

"Maybe some nutcase out there is. And maybe not. He might be gone forever. Or he might run us off the road as we go around the next bend."

"And your point?"

"We can't let something uncontrollable ruin our lives. Rafe, suppose we never figure this out? Then what?"

Rafe started the car. "We're wasting time."

"Wasting time?" Rhianna's scorn came out in a soft hiss of irritation. He thought he heard her mumble something about stubborn men who made decisions *for* women instead of *with* them, but he didn't ask her to speak up.

Again he'd said the wrong thing. Rafe had only one answer. Only one way to make things right. He had to figure out who was behind the kidnapping. Then and only then could he finalize things between himself and Rhianna.

A half hour later, as Rhianna remained abnormally quiet, Rafe talked his way into Judge Stuart's office by telling his secretary he'd made a last minute appointment with the judge and they'd arrived early. It wasn't difficult to pull off the lie since he'd known his secretary for years.

Rhianna seemed to have lost all interest in helping him. If she'd been cold before, she was freezing him out now. She didn't look around curiously, but slumped in a chair and ignored him.

Fine. He could search the place himself.

Rafe opened and closed several drawers of Judge

Stuart's desk without finding anything unusual. He checked a calendar for appointments, and a Rolodex, but found nothing incriminating. Turning to the file cabinets, he flipped through several drawers until he found one full of bank statements.

Rhianna finally came over to peer at the papers. "What are you looking at?"

"Bank statements for last month." He handed Rhianna a stack of envelopes. "See if there were any unusually large deposits made after we paid the ransom."

Rhianna let out a long sigh but took the folder to the desk and starting thumbing through the contents. She searched diligently, and he could have sworn she was relieved to have something to do. Obviously she didn't like the arguments between them any more than he did. And she needed to help.

Always ready to pitch in, always ready to offer suggestions, Rhianna was a woman he admired, respected and loved. So why was it so damn difficult to get along?

Exasperated, Rafe tried another file drawer but found nothing except trial notes and memos. Unwilling to leave without something to show for his efforts, he opened the last drawer. A file marked Sutton immediately caught his attention. He drew out a thick stack of papers.

Rhianna refiled the bank statements. "Nothing here. Find anything?"

Rafe shook his head. "These are a duplicate set of real estate documents outlining the terms of the loan payments. Dad has another copy in his office."

Suddenly several papers slipped loose. Rafe picked

them up, scanning quickly, ready to put them back in order. But one letter, a handwritten note from Judge Stuart to his attorney, outlining the terms of the agreement that he wanted the lawyer to draw up, drew Rafe's attention.

Suddenly Rafe noted the date and his hopes skyrocketed. "This is just what we needed." As he double-checked the date, his hand began to shake with anger and satisfaction. "We've got him."

"Who?" Rhianna looked from the closed door of the office back to Rafe, reminding him the secretary could come in at any time.

"Judge Stuart." Rafe spied a copy machine in the corner and flicked on the warm-up button. "In this letter, the judge instructs his attorney to draw up a document between the Suttons and himself."

"So?" Rhianna tossed her hair over her shoulder with impatience.

Rafe couldn't keep his whispered voice from rising with excitement. "The letter is dated two days *before* you were kidnapped."

Rhianna's expression changed from a puzzled frown to enlightenment. "If the judge knew your family would need a loan before anyone kidnapped me, then the man is a crook."

"Exactly." With immense satisfaction, Rafe placed the paper on the copy machine and pressed the start button. "This paper should provide enough evidence for the sheriff to obtain a search warrant."

"Search warrant?"

"To look on Stuart's premises for the ransom money or the stolen Rovells. He must have stashed the cash and the art away someplace safe, and that's why none of the marked bills have shown up.''

Elation thundered through Rafe. They had finally figured out who was behind their problems. The hardest part was over. Now that law enforcement officials would know where to look, it should be a simple matter of time until they nailed the judge.

A FEW HOURS LATER, Rafe and Rhianna sat facing Sheriff Demory and the senator over Rafe's dining table. Rhianna fed Allison a bottle, and despite her weariness, Rafe thought she looked beautiful. With an end to their difficulties finally in sight, he expected hope to shimmer in Rhianna's eyes, but instead he saw a lingering sadness. Would she ever forget what she'd been through? Or was she thinking of their uncertain future? When she caught him looking at her, she lifted her chin, squared her shoulders and gave him a dignified nod that made him want to fight all the harder for their cause.

The sheriff shook his head over the paper Rafe had handed him. ''This isn't enough to obtain a warrant.''

Rhianna's head jerked up, her eyes narrowed, but she didn't jostle the baby. ''What do you mean?''

''Well, there are two problems.'' The sheriff scratched his head. ''First, a year or two back, I deputized Rafe so he could legally help track down a criminal.''

Rhianna's brows drew together in puzzlement. ''I don't understand.''

''Rafe's snooping, the way he obtained this evidence, means it can't be used in a court of law. Any evidence obtained illegally is inadmissible in court.''

Rafe shook his head. "But that deputy thing was temporary."

"And even if we got past that little technicality—" the sheriff held up his hand to stop Rafe from talking "—I already called and spoke to Judge Stuart."

"He had a good excuse, I suppose?" Rhianna muttered.

The sheriff leaned forward and patted Rhianna's hand. "Stuart claims he simply wrote the wrong date on the note."

Rafe's blood heated as he struggled to keep his voice even. "That's ridiculous." He turned to his father. "What about the FBI? Can't they do something?"

The senator nodded his support just as Rafe knew he would. "You can be sure I'll push for action. But, Rafe, you must understand that Judge Stuart is a powerful man, with well-connected friends within the justice system. They will protect him, slow down the investigation, throw roadblocks in our way."

Sheriff Demory shrugged. "Without more evidence, I'm afraid we have nowhere to go."

"I have an idea." Rhianna said the words slowly. "Let's leak the story to the press."

The senator's eyes gleamed. "That's not a bad suggestion. If we shred Stuart's reputation, people will be less likely to help him."

Rafe held up the note with the judge's handwriting. "It would be better if we had more."

Rhianna let out a long, low sigh. "I think we should talk to the ex-Mrs. Stuart again. I have a feeling she might give us the ammunition we need."

Chapter Thirteen

The endless rain matched Rhianna's gloomy mood perfectly. Once again she'd left Allison with Laura to accompany Rafe to Denver. She detested the endless traveling. And despite the fact that talking to the judge's ex-wife was her own suggestion, she suspected it would prove futile. Rhianna figured that after the sheriff had called Stuart about the note in his file, the judge would have tidied up all the loose ends. Rhianna couldn't help feeling that the smart, well-connected and careful Judge Stuart had outwitted them from the beginning and might continue to do so.

She'd always believed that, once they discovered her kidnapper's identity, they'd be safe and the ranch would be saved. But she'd been wrong. The Suttons and Rhianna might now know their enemy's identity, but proving the man guilty might be impossible.

Even worse, Rhianna no longer bought Rafe's excuse that as long as the judge remained free to plot and plan against the Suttons, she would be in greater danger if they were married.

All last night, after she'd pointed out to Rafe that

she was already connected to the Suttons and there-
fore a target, she'd waited and waited for Rafe to
reassure her, to tell her that marriage wouldn't put her
in more danger than she was already in by having
borne his daughter. But he hadn't discussed the subject, and his silence had told her what she needed to
know. Rafe was using the judge as an excuse.
Rhianna didn't know Rafe's real reason—maybe he
didn't love her enough, maybe he didn't know himself—but she couldn't wait around forever. She had
her life to live, a daughter's future to consider.

Facing the possibility that the Suttons could never
prove the judge's guilt exhausted Rhianna. The
thought of losing Rafe left a black hollowness inside
her that hurt so much she didn't want to think about
it. But she had to think of tomorrow and the day after
that. She couldn't go on much longer, playing ama-
teur detective. Rafe might never realize or admit that
he was using Judge Stuart's threats as an excuse to
avoid marriage.

As Rafe parked in front of Karen Prescott's house
and slipped the keys into his pocket, Rhianna drank
in his stunning good looks. Dressed in a navy sports
coat, blue shirt and jeans, he could have modeled for
one of the rodeo magazines. He possessed a casual
elegance and grace, and an air of intelligence that
made him so sexy she had trouble remembering his
stubbornness. Rafe wasn't going to change his mind
about marriage—not even if they nailed the judge
cold.

And unless something new broke today, the Suttons
would lose their land. With the mortgage payment
due, time had finally run out. The insurance on the

stolen art was still tied up in an investigation. The blocked pass had been cleared, but not in time to round up and sell the cattle. Rhianna wasn't hopeful, but she vowed to press through this last interview before making a final decision about what to do next.

Karen Prescott answered her front door with an abrupt gesture. "Please, come in."

She led them into a sitting room decorated in pastels and flowers, offered them drinks, which they declined, then sat while Rafe told her his suspicions about the judge and about the note he'd found. While Rafe spoke, Rhianna watched the woman carefully. Several emotions crossed Karen's face, but surprise wasn't one of them.

"I'm not sure I can help you," Karen began.

Rafe spoke softly, persuasively, clearly understanding that the woman was stressed out by the conversation. "We'll keep whatever you can tell us in confidence."

So Rafe had also noticed that Karen was reluctant to talk about her ex-husband. Rhianna had always known Rafe could be charming and sensitive and kind, but she'd never seem him this compelling. It wasn't just his words but his demeanor, the casual tilt of his head, his slight lean forward to show Karen how important this information was to him. Rafe would have been a brilliant trial attorney, but Rhianna was glad he'd decided to breed horses instead. The Suttons had dealt with enough criminals to last three generations.

"I know nothing about my ex-husband's day-to-day activities. He was an extremely secretive man."

"Did he ever speak harshly about my father?" Rafe asked.

"Actually, he was consumed by everything your father accomplished, with a fervor I thought unhealthy."

"What do you mean?" Rhianna asked.

"The judge considered himself Senator Sutton's enemy, an arch rivalry that started in high school."

Rafe looked surprised. "High school?"

"Your father, a star quarterback, defeated Stuart's team, and Stuart never recovered from fumbling a catch that could have scored a touchdown and turned around the championship game."

Rhianna and Rafe exchanged a long glance, but neither interrupted Karen.

"Their rivalry escalated in the political arena. As you already know, the senator defeated my ex when they both ran for mayor, governor, then senator. The only rivalry your father ever lost to Stuart was over me." Karen paused. "I picked the wrong man. I was young, foolish."

Rhianna didn't know what to say. As usual, Rafe did. "I'm sure the judge was considered quite a catch back then. He's brilliant and ambitious, a combination ladies find irresistible. You mustn't blame yourself."

"I should have seen through the surface charm to the maliciousness beneath." Karen shrugged. "But I was fooled. When our marriage ended in a bitter divorce, the judge blamed the failure on Senator Sutton."

"Why?" Rafe asked.

"My husband was an expert on shifting blame to anyone but himself. In the judge's twisted mind, the senator must have lied to the constituents or they would have voted for my ex. The judge thought that if he'd been elected senator instead of your father, then we'd still be married.''

"He told you this?'' Rhianna asked, finding the entire idea hard to take in.

"I would have divorced him if he'd become president of the United States. It's possible our divorce pushed him over the edge. It wasn't that he loved me. But I represented his only success in his rivalry with the senator—because I married him. When I left, it compounded all the jealousy and bitterness he felt over the years.''

"You're sure?'' Rafe asked, gently prodding Karen for more information.

"I have no proof, but I lived with the man for thirty-three years and knew him well. Too well. Some men measure their accomplishments against their fathers or brothers. My ex measured himself against Senator Sutton. And the senator beat my husband in every way that counted. He had five sons, a huge ranch, wealth, prestige. When the judge didn't measure up, he obsessed over how to beat the senator. Remember the baby-sitter that murdered Dr. Cameron Sutton's first wife?''

"What about her?''

"I heard the judge recommend the baby-sitter for the job. And all the while, he knew about her unstable background, knew she might cause trouble for Cam and his wife.''

Rafe spoke slowly, obviously putting together the pieces. "The judge was also partners with the lawyer who caused Chase and Laura all that trouble.''

"Exactly. I'm not surprised my ex may have turned to illegal means, for winning is everything to him. He's a bitter, lonely man and he obtains pleasure from watching others suffer."

Rhianna winced as she realized Rafe had been right all along. Judge Stuart had meticulously and ruthlessly planned to bring down the Suttons, stomping on anyone in the family, taking his revenge on the senator, his children and grandchildren. With a sinking feeling in her stomach, Rhianna knew that Karen had just confirmed the reason Rafe had given for not marrying her. As long as the judge went free, Rafe would never marry Rhianna, for fear that Stuart would go after her again.

He'd gone after Rhianna because she was the mother of Rafe's child. Being single hadn't protected her in the past. It wouldn't in the future. Rafe was simply using the judge as an excuse to avoid commitment.

He stood and paced the small sitting area. "All of this explains your ex-husband's motivations, but we need something more solid."

"Sorry, I can't help you there."

Rafe stopped and rested his hands on the back of the chair he'd vacated. "We need to find the marked bills used for the ransom. Or the stolen art."

"He hasn't spent the cash," Rhianna told Karen, forcing her thoughts to focus on the money, when she really wanted to make Rafe face up to the real reason he'd avoided marriage. "Have you any idea where he might have hidden the money or the artwork?"

Karen shook her head. "I have no idea."

"Did the judge keep a safety deposit box?' Rafe asked.

"I don't think so."

Rhianna closed her eyes for a brief moment, knowing this might be the last time she and Rafe ever worked together. That amount of cash had to take up a lot of space. "Does he have a safe at his house?"

"Not unless he installed one since I moved out."

Rafe swung the chair around and straddled it. "Does he have a hunting cabin?"

"No, but we have a ski chalet. And he doesn't ski. I used to think he kept a mistress there, but he was never interested in other women."

"Then why did he keep the place?" Rhianna asked, wondering if she'd ever understand the wealthy.

"The judge used the place to entertain men who funded his political campaigns. The monthly liquor and cigar bills could have fed a family of four for a year."

Rhianna could see that Rafe was ready to head off to the ski chalet in hopes of finding the ransom money stashed there. But she didn't believe the judge would be foolish enough to leave the money where they could find it. For all they knew, he had burned the cash and art—because it was the Sutton land he wanted.

Well, Judge Stuart wasn't going to steal that land. Rhianna had always known she might have to make this choice. She'd hoped and prayed that Rafe and she could somehow work things out. But too much stood in their way.

Rhianna could stop the judge. But to do so she

would lose everything she held dear. Everything that was important to her. Absolutely everything.

RHIANNA TOLD RAFE she had a headache, and asked him to drop her off at a Denver hotel. Although he'd been eager to search the judge's ski chalet, he'd accompanied her to the room and had room service bring her some aspirin.

Rafe patted the bed. "Lie down. Let me rub your head and maybe you'll feel well enough to accompany me."

Was that suspicion she heard in his tone? Or did she simply feel guilty for what she was about to do? Lying on the bed and closing her eyes, she tried to hurry Rafe on his way. "You really should go. Maybe you'll find the money in time to pay off the mortgage and put the judge away for good."

Rafe rubbed just above her ears with his thumbs. "Maybe. If not, Hal Stone made your father and me an offer on Sweetness."

"Oh, Rafe. Losing that foal would hurt my father as much as losing the Sutton ranch would hurt the senator. We can't let Stuart win. You should go now."

His eyes were haunted with shadows of quicksilver. "I don't like leaving you alone."

"I'll be fine." She grabbed his hand and did her best to look him straight in the eyes. "Please go, Rafe. You only have a few hours."

"Okay, okay." He held up his cell phone. "Call me if you need me."

She nodded, memorizing the way he looked at her this last time.

Rafe hesitated at the door and turned back. "Wish me luck."

She gave him a thumb's-up.

"Chain the door behind me."

Rhianna nodded past the lump in her throat. This was goodbye. That Rafe didn't know it didn't make letting him go any easier. He would never feel the same way about her again—not after what she was about to do. She told herself it didn't matter. Rafe was strong. He had his family. And she—she would know she'd put things right.

Rhianna's decision to leave Rafe left her shaking and sick at heart. But what she did right now could prevent the senator and his sons from losing their ranch. Rafe and her father could keep Sweetness. Allison would have her heritage. Rhianna's daughter would grow up in a family surrounded by aunts and uncles and cousins and a father who loved her. Because Rhianna had just made the most painful decision of her life—to leave her precious baby with Rafe.

He closed the door behind him, and the tears she'd held back streamed down Rhianna's cheeks. She angrily wiped them aside. She could cry buckets of tears later. She might never stop. But now she had to be stronger than she'd ever been.

Rhianna didn't bother locking the door. Ruthlessly, she pushed her sobs into a dark place inside her, imprisoned the pain, reached for the phone. She had to do this now—before she lost her courage.

Her hands shook as she dialed the number. Her stomach churned. "Duncan?"

"Changed your mind?"

"Yes." Duncan hadn't bothered with a greeting,

and she responded with a coldness that matched her soul. At least she had the knowledge that Duncan wasn't her kidnapper. Duncan needn't know that she was doing this for love—love for her daughter. And love for Rafe Sutton, whom she could never blame for being the way he was. Rafe had always been honest with Rhianna. He'd told her from the start he wasn't the marrying kind. And while he might eventually propose because they shared a child together, Rhianna wouldn't marry him for the wrong reasons. While she would deal with Duncan as a business partner, she could never have done that with Rafe. She couldn't bear to marry Rafe, then watch their affection for one another change first to resentment and then hatred. Better to make a clean break now and ensure her daughter's future.

Marrying Duncan for the wrong reasons bothered her much less. Duncan didn't love her—she wasn't sure he was capable of loving anyone. He just didn't want to lose her. He never lost in business and he wasn't about to lose at romance. She suspected he wanted her like he wanted the Picasso on his living room wall or the Rolls Royce he parked next to his Lamborghini. To him their arrangement was practical. Her emotions wouldn't be ravaged if Duncan's attentions or feelings toward her ever changed.

Rhianna took a deep breath. "I'll marry you this afternoon."

Duncan didn't ask unnecessary questions. He'd pull some strings or bribe an official to arrange the necessary paperwork in time to marry within hours. Somehow, Rhianna got through the rest of the conversation. She told Duncan the name of her hotel and her room number, that she would order a dress and that he should bring a notary to marry them and a check to pay off the Sutton mortgage. The only surprise had been when Duncan told her she would need to sign a prenuptial agreement, claiming she was already getting enough cash out of him to last a lifetime. If she chose to squander the money on the Suttons, that was her decision.

And Rhianna agreed. Hanging up, she dropped her face into her hands. Somehow, she would go on without seeing her daughter every day. Without seeing Rafe every day. Knowing they were well and safe and together, living the life they should have, would sustain Rhianna through the endless empty days and nights ahead. The sacrifice she would make today was the right one. She knew in her heart she was doing what was best, but why did it have to hurt so much?

RAFE WORRIED ABOUT Rhianna as he took the hotel elevator down to the lobby. She'd never mentioned the word *migraine,* but the agony he'd seen when he looked into her eyes had been much worse than her casual tone had indicated. He didn't want to leave her. Suppose she needed medical attention?

Suppose she died?

Died?

Where had that thought come from? Rhianna was a young, healthy woman. Two aspirin could cure her headache.

Aspirin won't cure a brain aneurism.

She'll be fine.

Maybe. You want to take the chance?

Did he? Rafe shook off the fear for Rhianna as he

exited the elevator and strode across the lobby. He needed to check Stuart's ski chalet for the ransom money. And he needed to call the senator, but his cell phone battery was dead.

Rafe stopped at the bank of phones in the lobby, plucked a quarter from his pocket and tried his dad's cell phone. The senator answered on the first ring. "Yes?"

"Judge Stuart's ex-wife confirmed that he's been after you for a long time. Apparently, he blamed his loss to you in the senate race for the break-up of his marriage. He wants revenge, but we still need proof."

"My contacts at the FBI say the judge is clean."

Rafe heard weary frustration in the senator's voice, but not defeat. His father would fight for his lands to his last breath. "Any luck on moving the cattle through the pass?"

"It's slow going."

"I'm heading up to the judge's ski chalet—"

"That might not be a good idea. The judge could be waiting up there…with a gun."

"He's in court today. I checked."

"Sounds like you have things under control. But be careful. Keep Rhianna safe."

The senator often told his sons to keep their women safe. Rafe wondered if his father felt guilty because he hadn't been there for Rafe's mother. The senator had been working the night she'd died, returning home far too late to help his wife, whom Rafe had found dead on the kitchen floor. Although the senator rarely mentioned how much he missed his wife, or spoke of the heart attack that had dropped her while she cooked supper, he often reminded his sons to take care of their families, and he never stopped telling them to take care of one another.

"I love you, Dad. Gotta go." Rafe hung up the phone and hesitated. What had made him think about his mother just now? Was it his worry over Rhianna? Rhianna wasn't going to die on him like his mother. Rhianna just had a headache.

Until his wife's death, the senator hadn't even known his wife had a heart condition. But Rafe knew Rhianna was hurting.

His father had had no warning.

Sweat beaded on Rafe's brow. He had to leave Rhianna, search the ski chalet. He had only hours left. He walked past the hotel boutique, saw a clerk taking a white gown off a mannequin. Through the open door, he heard the woman say, "Room 567."

Rhianna's room. Why would she buy a fancy white dress when she had a headache? It didn't make sense. Maybe he had mistaken the room number.

Rafe stepped into the boutique. "Room 567 is mine. I'll take the dress up."

The salesgirl smiled at him. "The groom isn't supposed to see the wedding dress before—"

"Wedding dress?" Just what the hell was going on? His heart did a triple somersault. Rafe hadn't proposed to Rhianna, so why would she be buying a dress she hadn't even tried on?

"The wedding's at four o'clock. The dress has to be up there in half an hour. Relax, sir. We have everything under control."

A wedding at four o'clock? Today? Suddenly Rafe understood. Rhianna didn't have a headache. She'd wanted him out of the way because she was getting married—but not to him.

Damn her! What the hell was she doing? Rafe didn't bother waiting for the elevator. He slammed through the stairwell door and took the stairs three at a time, his anger building with every leap upward.

Racing down the hall, he slid to a stop before the door, fumbled with the key, then burst into the room, feeling betrayed and angry and very, very riled.

Rhianna spun to face him, the makeup she'd been applying dropping from her hand. Quickly she knelt and scooped up her compact. "Forget something?"

"My wedding invitation." Anger and pride made his voice rough and harsh. "Here I was worried about your headache, and you're planning to leave me to marry another man. Don't you think you owe me an explanation?"

She flinched as if he'd struck her, but she raised her chin. "I don't owe you anything."

"Just what the hell do you think you're doing?"

Rhianna pointedly looked at her watch. "Don't you have to search the ski chalet?"

How could she be so calm? Why did her expression look so brittle, as if she'd shatter into a thousand pieces if he touched her?

All his pent-up anger seeped out of him as he realized the pain he'd seen before had not been from a headache but from inner turmoil. She hadn't made this decision easily. And she'd made it alone, without even hinting to him what she intended. That hurt as if she'd flayed his nerves. Now that he looked at her puffy, slightly red eyes, he suspected she'd been crying. And there could be only one reason for her tears. "You're going to marry Duncan?"

"Yes."

Rafe didn't understand her. Didn't know how she could tear them apart without even discussing her plans with him. "And take my daughter?"

"I'll give you full custody of Allison."

Her words floored him. She'd spoken with no intonation, but he could imagine what they had cost her. He might doubt her feelings for him, but he could never doubt her love for their daughter. Rafe had been there when Allison had been born, had seen Rhianna's joy when she'd first held their child, listened as she'd sung lullabies and kissed her goodnight.

Shocked by her decision, Rafe stared at her with confusion. And then her reasons hit him. "You're marrying Duncan because he agreed to pay off the debt, aren't you? The land isn't worth it. Are you out of your mind?"

Rhianna sat down and began to apply her makeup. "It's better this way. The Suttons will keep the ranch. You and my father will keep Sweetness."

"And what about Allison?"

"She'll grow up fine. You're a wonderful father."

"She needs a mother."

"We've always known she couldn't have both of us. At least this way, she'll keep her heritage. And Duncan doesn't want her. She's better off with you."

She had it all figured out. "And what about us?"

"There is no us." Her voice cracked, but sounded final. Rafe wasn't buying it.

"You don't love me?" Rafe asked, his disbelief plain in his voice.

"I'm moving on."

"You don't believe that I love you?" he guessed.

"Actually, I think you do."

"Let me get this straight. I love you. You love me. We have a child together. And you're going to marry another man?"

She waved him away with her hand. "If you wanted to fight for us, you'd hurry to the ski chalet and find the money. The judge would go to jail and then I wouldn't have to marry Duncan."

"You know damn well I'd never even get there before you and Duncan exchanged vows." She thought he could walk away. Lose her. God! How could he live with himself if he lost her? How could he tell Allison her parents had never married because her father was a coward? "You aren't getting rid of me so easily."

Her bottom lip quivered. "Why are you determined to make this so difficult? Go away. I'm going to marry Duncan."

"I don't think so."

She looked up at him and alarm entered her eyes. "Rafe, be sensible—"

"Sensible?" He grabbed her wrist and pulled her to her feet. Her chest slammed against his, and he cradled her firmly but gently against him. "I won't let you marry him. I won't let another man marry the woman I love."

Chapter Fourteen

Rafe's arms around her felt so good that Rhianna wanted to lean into him, rest her head under his chin and take comfort in his warmth. She didn't dare stay so close, breathing in his masculine scent, touching his heat, for fear she'd never find the courage to leave.

She drew back from his arms and immediately felt cold. "You won't *let* me marry Duncan? I don't believe that decision is yours to make."

Rafe took her hand and drew her down next to him on the bed, so they sat side by side. "I never wanted to marry, but I didn't know why. Until I met you, I never looked for a reason."

"I'm no longer buying the-woman-I-marry-will-be-in-danger theory," Rhianna warned him.

"You're too smart for that. But for a while, I really did think that someone was after my family, and I wanted you to be safe." Rafe shoved his fingers through his hair and looked at her calmly, but with an intensity that zinged straight to her heart. "I did have good reasons. The judge does want to ruin the Suttons."

"But—"

"Let me get this out while I can." Rafe squeezed her hand, seemingly determined to tell her more, something he didn't like to speak about. "When I was six, I was playing with some toys under the kitchen table while my mother fixed dinner. One minute she was standing up, and the next, she'd collapsed on the floor, and the onions she had been cooking started to burn. I still hate the smell of onions."

"Where were your brothers?" Rhianna asked gently.

"In the old barn with Dad. Back then it was a good ten-minute drive from there to the house."

No wonder he considered the barn a safe haven. Rhianna didn't need a psychiatry degree to realize the young Rafe had wished to be safe in the barn with his brothers and father. "No one else was in the house?"

Rafe shook his head. "I didn't know what to do. I dialed 911, then yelled for Dad on the radio, but I didn't want to leave Mom. I kept trying to wake her, but I knew. I'd seen dead cows. I knew she was... gone. Dad heard me and drove like a race car driver. It seemed like the longest minutes of my life, but not even Dad could save her." Rafe paused. "It was the only time I saw him cry—until my oldest brother was killed. And then I watched Chase grieve when Laura left him, watched Cam grieve over the loss of his first wife and I..."

"You what? Thought it would be better never to love anyone?"

He didn't answer for a long time. But finally the words came in a harsh rasp. "I thought if I loved you, married you—that you would die."

Like his mother. Like his eldest brother, Brent. Like his sister-in-law. Rafe had seen more than his share of death and it had marked him. Rhianna could hear the truth in his voice, see the fear in his eyes.

She squeezed Rafe's hand. "I'm still here."

"I'm glad." Rafe paused. "I tried to deny what I felt for you. But I can't. You mean too much to me."

"My dying prematurely isn't a rational fear, Rafe," she tried to reassure him.

"To me, it is." He turned to her then. "But I would rather face the fear, live with it, beat it, than lose you to another man."

She heard the strength in his words, read the determination in his eyes, and the weight pressing on her heart lightened. Time might heal the old wounds. And Rhianna hadn't given him enough time to overcome his past. "I'm glad you told me, but it doesn't change anything."

Rafe jerked to his feet and then spun slowly to face her. "What do you mean?"

"I'm still going to marry Duncan."

Rafe's eyes narrowed. He looked to be two seconds away from shaking her. "Why?"

"Because too many people's futures depend on my actions. Duncan will pay off the mortgage—"

"You're more important than the Sutton lands."

"And you and my father will have the chance to raise Sweetness."

"Look, Rhianna. When your father thought you were in danger, he was willing to sell Sweetness. Don't you think he'd do the same to ensure your happiness? My family can survive without the acreage. Dad has his sights on the White House and spends most of his time in Washington. Chase and Laura can live at the Embry place, which her parents own. Tyler can foreman any ranch. I can always practice law.''

"You'd hate that.''

"I'd rather my daughter had her mother.'' Rafe tugged at her hand. "And if we weren't wasting all this time arguing, we might find the money and this conversation would be irrelevant.''

Rhianna tried to free her hand from Rafe's as he pulled her toward the door. "Where are you taking me?''

Rafe never answered. He flung open the door and found Duncan Phillips standing there. "Sorry, your bride's changed her mind.''

Before Duncan could say a word, Rafe pulled her down the hallway. But Duncan was not a man who gave up easily. He spun on his heel and jogged after them, catching up just as Rafe yanked Rhianna into the elevator.

Duncan stepped in after them. He looked from Rafe to Rhianna and sneered. "What's going on?''

Rafe started to say something and Rhianna kicked his shin. Duncan might be cold, he might be selfish, but he deserved to be let down as gently as possible. "I'm sorry, Duncan. Rafe would rather lose the ranch than me. And I'm not sure if I could really give up my daughter.''

Duncan rocked back on his heels, folded his arms over his chest and surveyed her from head to toe. Rhianna realized her eyes were still puffy from crying, she hadn't finished applying her makeup and her hair probably looked like she'd stepped off the set of a Halloween movie.

Duncan blew out air through his nose. "Maybe it's for the best. You might never have learned to behave suitably."

Beside her in the elevator, Rafe bristled, but when she picked up her foot to kick his shin again, he relaxed and let Rhianna handle Duncan.

"You deserve a better woman than me, but I am sorry for inconveniencing you," she said.

The elevator stopped, and they exited. Duncan, looking none too upset, tipped his hat at the first pretty woman in the lobby. Rhianna suspected he'd recover from his disappointment almost immediately, but she still felt badly for leading him on—but not as badly as if she'd had to endure marriage to him.

Meanwhile Rafe hurried her into his car. He plunked his cell phone into the recharger as she checked the clock on the dash. They'd never make the drive to the chalet before dark. Time to pay the mortgage had run out. She settled in the car next to Rafe, who'd been strangely quiet since the scene at the hotel. He acted almost as if confronting his past and the deaths in his family had surprised him as much as it had her.

She couldn't blame him for avoiding such unpleasant memories. But she also wondered if just recognizing his reluctance could help him get over them. Rhianna might have canceled her wedding with Duncan, but she couldn't live with Rafe forever without some kind of formal commitment. She wouldn't do that to Allison. But she also owed it to her daughter to give Rafe time to work out his past. And that also meant giving herself to him freely, giving them what they both wanted—a chance to grow closer and let their passions blossom.

AT TEN TO FIVE, Rafe pulled up in front of the ski chalet. Rhianna and Rafe could never search the huge contemporary A-frame in the ten minutes they had left.

Rafe took out his cell phone and called his dad. "We're here. Why don't you wait until the banks close, then overnight a check to the judge in case we find the cash?"

And if they failed, the check would bounce. But Rafe had just bought them more time to search the chalet, because the check only had to be posted in today's mail—not cashed by the judge.

So the search still loomed in front of them. Before they'd left Karen, she'd told them the judge hid a key in the third planter to the right of the front door. Rafe found the key easily, let them inside and punched the security code into the alarm system, while Rhianna held her breath. If the judge had changed the code since his divorce, the silent alarm would call the police. But the blinking red light changed to solid green, indicating Rafe had successfully deactivated the system.

It turned dark early in the mountains, and in the dim interior, Rhianna couldn't see much until after Rafe flipped on the lights. A huge stone fireplace dominated one wall. Turquoise leather couches with plum-colored pillows formed a seating group around a marble table and a multicolored, contemporary rug. The rest of the floor was bare wood that creaked as they walked across it.

"Where do we start?" Rhianna asked in a whisper, reluctant to leave Rafe's side. Even with the lights on, the house spooked her. Just knowing the judge owned the property lent the place a sinister air. She kept expecting him to pop out of a dark corner, pointing a gun at them for trespassing.

"Let's look around downstairs, but I'm betting he'd hide the money in an area most guests wouldn't go to—like his bedroom."

"Maybe he has a wall safe."

"It'd have to be huge. Two duffel bags worth of cash take up a lot of room."

Rhianna followed Rafe into a spotless kitchen of gleaming stainless steel and deep green countertops. "One thing I don't understand."

"What?"

"If we find the money, what will you do?" She looked over at Rafe as he peered into a well-stocked freezer. "Sheriff Demory said he can't use the evidence in court if we find it illegally. And we don't have the judge's permission to be here."

Rafe dug through a pile of frozen chickens, steaks and bacon. "I haven't forgotten." He seemed satisfied the money wasn't there and closed the freezer, moving on to the walk-in pantry.

Despite the pantry's size, the money could hardly be hidden behind the canned food and other supplies on the shelves, and Rafe quickly searched the cabinets. They inspected the entire downstairs and finally ascended a staircase to the second level. Rhianna unbuttoned her jacket and followed Rafe into a guest room with a sinking feeling in her gut.

She'd never believed they would find the money,

but felt obligated to help Rafe search. While he looked under the bed and behind pictures, she checked the closet.

Nothing.

They skipped the four guest rooms and entered the owner's suite. The master bedroom occupied the entire third floor and boasted a walk-in closet, a separate exercise area, a study and a huge bathroom. They looked through empty suitcases in the closet, a trunk by the foot of the bed, and Rafe even pulled down the stairs to the attic. Maybe the Rovells would be up there.

It was empty.

Rhianna swept her hair off her face and looked at Rafe. ''Houses like this don't have basements, do they?''

''Nope. But there's the guest bedrooms and a garage we haven't searched yet.''

They found nothing in the guest bedrooms, so trudged downstairs, and with every step Rhianna's discouragement grew. She couldn't believe anyone would leave the cash just lying around, especially someone as smart as Judge Stuart.

After checking inside the washer and dryer, Rafe opened the laundry room door to the garage. Rhianna saw a sedan, a minivan and three skimobiles. All the toys of a wealthy man accustomed to entertaining on the highest levels. While she checked the vehicles and the sedan's trunk, Rafe opened the seats of the skimobiles. Several bicycles rested against a water heater wrapped in blankets for insulation against Colorado's harsh winters, but she saw nothing that could be used to hide cash—no boxes or trash cans.

Rafe eyed the bikes and walked toward them, and she followed wearily. As much as she wanted to return to the ranch and hold Allison, she hated to go back knowing they had failed.

Rafe plucked at duct tape that held the blanket around the hot water heater. He moved the bikes, and she rolled them away and leaned them against one wall. "What is it?"

"That blanket around the water heater is awfully thick."

"It must get really cold here in winter."

"Yeah."

Rafe pulled loose the duct tape, then reached behind the blanket. And pulled out a bundle of cash.

He let out a whoop and fanned the money in her face.

Rhianna's heart pounded with excitement. "You found it."

"We have to be sure." Rafe pulled out a cigarette lighter and heated a hundred-dollar bill. "If the ink turns blue, this is the marked cash used to pay the ransom, and the serial numbers will match the FBI's list."

Rhianna held her breath. Rafe had to be careful. He had to heat the paper without burning it. The judge could have laundered the money, somehow exchanging the marked bills for clean ones. If they had just found money that couldn't be traced to the ransom, their work would have gone for nothing.

As Rafe continued to hold the lighter near the paper, she peered at the bill. "It's turning blue!" She threw her arms around Rafe and kissed him. "You did it."

He kissed her back with enough heat to warm her to her toes, and then yanked the rest of the blanket away, exposing neatly stacked piles of cash. "Go get two of the suitcases upstairs."

Rhianna frowned. "Aren't we calling the cops?"

Rafe shook his head. "We found this money doing an illegal search."

"So what are you going to do?"

Rafe grinned in triumph. "Give this money to the judge."

"What? We're stealing this money?"

"Yep. But don't worry. We'll give it back when we pay off the mortgage. Kind of ironic, don't you think?"

"But—but is he going to get away with kidnapping me?"

Rafe gathered her into his arms. "He may not go to jail, but he's going to lose everything that matters to him. His job, his reputation, his friends. We'll leak the story to the press later and he can't sue for slander since we'll be telling the truth."

Rhianna supposed she'd have to be satisfied, but a shiver of fear marred her excitement over their success. Would she ever really feel safe unless the judge was behind bars?

RAFE ZIPPED THE CASH inside two suitcases and locked them in the trunk of his car. Then he and Rhianna headed for Denver, since he had one important stop to make on the way home. He didn't want to rush, didn't want to fly.

Without telling Rhianna his intentions, Rafe parked in front of the bank. Thanks to his father's connec-

tions, the bank president met him at the door even
though it was way past normal banking hours.

Two security guards lifted the suitcases and carried
them into the vault, while a photographer from a Denver paper took pictures that would headline the
judge's disgrace on tomorrow's front page. The senator had seen to it that the story would make national
news. The judge would be forced to resign in disgrace.

Rafe signed the necessary paperwork, took
Rhianna's hand, then turned to the bank president. "I
appreciate your opening up for us. There's one more
item on my agenda. Would you mind if we looked
inside the family box?"

The bank president nodded. "Not at all." He held
out his hand. "Your key, please."

Rafe handed him the key to the Sutton vault and
led Rhianna to their private box, while she eyed him
curiously. Rafe pretended not to notice, nor did he
explain. He just was grateful she didn't ask questions.

The president used a bank key in one lock, Rafe's
key in the other. He pulled out the box and handed it
to Rafe. "You can use the desk over there."

Rafe, still holding Rhianna's hand, led her to the
private area the man had indicated. He opened the
box and retrieved a black velvet jewelry pouch.
Rhianna looked from the pouch to Rafe, but didn't
say anything, no doubt thinking he was simply bringing his father a trinket. Rafe slipped the pouch into
his pocket and returned the box to its place in the
vault, where the bank president relocked it.

Fifteen minutes later, they were on their way to an
exclusive hotel between Denver and Highview. Rafe

had picked the most romantic location he could think of for their evening, and hoped Rhianna would be pleased. While she'd freshened up in the bank's rest room, he'd put his cell phone to good use.

Excitement thrummed through Rafe, and he didn't feel the least bit tired. He wanted to drink champagne and celebrate. He wanted to twirl Rhianna around in his arms and spend the night together without the worry of losing the ranch. They'd defeated Judge Stewart, and though the man might not do jail time, he'd lose much of his influence and power. If he ever tried to threaten the Suttons again, Rafe would be there to stop him. Rafe still feared for Rhianna's safety, but he'd rather live with her and his fears than without her.

As they drove along the highway, Rhianna cocked her head to the side, watching him with a slight smile. "You have a mischievous gleam in your eyes."

"Do I?"

"Umm." She crossed one leg lazily over the other. "I suppose we aren't driving all the way back tonight?"

"I can't wait that long."

"Can't wait that long for what?"

"To have you."

Her eyes darkened, and her voice turned husky. "Do I have something you want?"

If she wasn't careful, he wouldn't make it to the luxurious hotel room he'd reserved. "You have lots of things that I want."

"Like what?"

"Just that you're you."

Now that was real eloquent, he chastised himself,

but then realized she looked like a cat who'd just feasted on a bowl of whipped cream.

She fluffed her hair over her shoulder, and the scent of her shampoo made him realize how accustomed he'd become to the little nuances that added up to Rhianna. But it wasn't just her scent or the taste of her lush lips that made him forget every vow he'd ever made, it was her undaunted spirit. He'd never forget her willingness to give up her own happiness to protect their daughter's future. Rhianna's love was selfless and deeper than he deserved.

"Rafe?" she asked, interrupting his thoughts.

"Yeah?"

"What did you take out of the bank vault?"

"It's a surprise."

"For whom?" she asked, and he realized she didn't have a clue how much he had changed since this afternoon, when he'd thought he might lose her to Duncan.

"Hold on a second. We're here." Rafe pulled into the hotel without answering Rhianna's question.

"Where?"

"It's a private spa. The owner is a friend of Cam's. While the minimum stay is a week, if they have an empty cabin, he lets the family use it. This is the first time I've been here."

Minutes later, an efficient member of the staff had unlocked a door to their own private cabin and ushered them inside. "Dinner will be delivered in half an hour."

Rhianna's eyes widened at the art deco furnishings. A fire crackled merrily in the fireplace. Vases of fresh flowers lent the room an aromatic scent. A box of chocolates sat on the counter next to a bowl of fruit.

Rhianna sank into a plush chair and kicked off her shoes. "I'll flip you for the shower."

Rafe tugged her to her feet. "Come on. We'll share."

To their surprise, the bathroom didn't have a shower. Instead a luxurious acrylic bathtub with jets sat on a podium overlooking a glass-enclosed terrace. Through the window, a full moon was just rising over a mountain peak.

While Rhianna lit the candles surrounding the tub, Rafe adjusted the water. She shyly turned out the lights before stripping off her clothes. She looked magnificent in the candlelight, and Rafe hurriedly removed his clothes to join her. But not before removing a certain item of jewelry from its pouch.

He slipped into the steaming water and snuggled next to Rhianna. She wrapped one leg over his to keep from floating away. "I could get used to this."

He draped one arm over her shoulder. "Could you get used to me?"

"I suppose I already have." She tilted her head at a cocky angle and teased, "It wasn't easy, either."

"Is that so?"

"You can be quite demanding." His hand curved around her breast. "Greedy, really." She arched into him and let her hand do some wandering of its own. When she discovered how ready he was to be greedy, she chuckled with pleasure. "Oh, my. You're really going to have to control yourself, darling. They're delivering dinner soon."

Rafe spied a phone conveniently placed next to the

tub. Lazily, he picked up the receiver and dialed room service. "Could you please delay our meal another hour?"

Rafe didn't even wait for an answer. Rhianna's hands were too busy roaming all over him. If he didn't slow her down, she wouldn't be in the right position for his surprise. Slowly he shifted until he knelt between her open thighs. When he didn't immediately reach for her, she looked at him with a fierce longing.

He ached to crush her to him, but refused to act like a heathen. A man of his age could restrain himself—especially for the woman he loved. Rafe kissed Rhianna's forehead, her nose, her chin.

"You're driving me wild," she complained when he refused to deepen his kiss.

"I like you wild." He tilted up her chin. "And I like you calm. I like you angry, and happy, and everything in between. In case you haven't noticed, I'm crazy about you."

"Oh, I've noticed." She reached between his legs and caressed the length of him.

"Have you also noticed that I can't stop thinking about you? Noticed that I don't want to stop thinking about you? You've bewitched me."

Rhianna chuckled. "If you're calling me a witch, I'll take that as a compliment."

"What I want to call you...is wife." He whipped out the huge emerald that had been his mother's and accidentally dropped it between her legs.

"Did you say wife?" Rhianna sputtered. "We have to get married for me to be a wife."

"I've heard that's the way it's done."

Face flushed, breasts floating enticingly, she leaned back against the edge of the tub and laced her hands behind her head. ''Are you sure?''

''I'm scared to death of doing this wrong. You *are* going to say yes?''

''Was that a ring you dropped?''

''It was.''

''Well, I think you should find it and place it on my finger.''

''I'll take that as a yes.'' Rafe whooped in pleasure and started to gather her into his arms. But she remained plastered with her back against the tub, her voice husky. ''I believe that ring fell in a very delicate place. It'll probably take you a while to find it.''

So the lady wanted to play games, did she? Rafe couldn't have been more pleased. He intended to take a very, very, very long time finding that ring.

Chapter Fifteen

The wedding had gone off without a hitch, and Rhianna looked radiant as she danced at the reception in Rafe's arms. Laughter warmed her eyes. Rafe didn't mind when she missed a few steps as she blew kisses at Allison and the senator every time they danced by.

Life had settled into a comfortable pattern of working with Rhianna and her father, who had moved to Highview. Sweetness showed the promise of a champion. The Rovells had been found unharmed in an abandoned truck alongside the highway and the Suttons had donated them to the museum in their mother's name. Seeing Rhianna for breakfast, lunch and dinner and most of the hours between helped Rafe ease his fears over her safety.

The judge had seemingly disappeared after resigning when the scandal hit the newspapers. National networks picked up the story and shredded Judge Stuart's character so that he would never hold another job as a public servant. Still, Rafe longed for justice. He wanted the man behind bars. He wanted to know his family was safe.

Rhianna leaned forward and nipped Rafe's shoulder. The slight pain brought him back to the sounds of music and clapping hands, and the sight of his smiling bride. But she had an air of seriousness in her eyes as she looked up at him. "Having regrets already?"

Rafe vowed to hide his thoughts more carefully. He wanted nothing to spoil their wedding day, and Rhianna was too good at guessing what he was thinking. He kissed her lightly on the lips, then twirled her around the makeshift dance floor, which the hands had set up under the tent in the senator's backyard. "My only regret is that we didn't do this sooner."

"The men in your family seem to have their babies first, marriage second," Rhianna teased.

"I'm the exception." Cam tapped Rafe on the shoulder and cut in, but spoke loudly enough to tease the groom. "But then Alexa says I'm exceptional. *I* made it to the altar before I had the twins."

Rafe moved aside and let his brother dance with Rhianna. "That's because you don't think, you process—like a damn computer chip."

Rafe missed Cam's comeback, but it must of been a doozy because Rhianna's peal of laughter drifted back to him. He headed for Allison, who seemed quite content in the crook of her grandfather's arm.

Rafe smiled down at his daughter. "Looks as if you have things under control," he said to his dad.

The senator nodded. "I like babies. And with Chase and Laura's two kids, Cam's twins and now Allison, I'm getting lots of practice." The senator's gaze drifted to Tyler, who stood with his back to a wall, leaning lightly on a cane. The daughter of one of the ranch hands was trying to tug him onto the dance floor, but Tyler kept refusing.

"He's resisting awfully hard," Rafe commented.

"Won't do him any good when the right woman comes along." The senator shifted Allison to his shoulder, but his gaze remained on Tyler. "I just hope I'm still around when he falls in love. Mark my words, he's going to fall hard and be more stubborn about it than the rest of you put together."

How like his father to want them all married off while he alone remained single. Rafe spied a local female real estate agent eyeing the senator as if he were a prime piece of property, so Rafe took Allison from his father. He winked good luck to the woman and twirled Allison onto the dance floor.

"Come on, sweetheart. Let's find your mama." Rafe stepped lightly among the dancers and heard a commotion on the edge of the crowd. At first, he figured one of the cowhands had had too much to drink.

But the music suddenly stopped. People screamed. Some fled.

Cradling Allison in his arms, Rafe shouldered his way through the crowd. Several gasps warned him that something was very wrong. Wildly he looked right, then left for Rhianna. Instead, he spied Laura, and placed the baby in his sister-in-law's capable hands.

At the sound of a scream, Rafe spun and his blood froze. Judge Stuart had crashed the reception. He stood, holding a knife to Rhianna's throat. Rhianna's face had turned as pale as her beaded dress, but her green eyes blazed with anger as much as fear.

As a trickle of blood dripped down her neck and

stained her gown, Rafe stepped forward, his blood boiling with anger. "Let her go."

Tyler tapped forward from the judge's right. "You heard my brother, let her go."

Chase edged in from the left. "You don't want to add murder to the charges against you."

"Don't tell me what I want," Judge Stuart snapped, his mouth a sneer, his eyes gloating. "Every last Sutton is going to die from the explosives I've set in this tent."

Rafe could see a glimmer of madness in the judge's eyes. Apparently the man's loss of face had been more than his tortured mind could stand. But what turned Rafe's fright to pure horror was the dynamite strapped to the judge's chest. He clearly intended to blow up everyone, himself included.

Suddenly the senator stepped out of the crowd. "It's me you want. Let everyone else go."

From out of the crowd, Cam let out a roar and socked the senator in the chin. The senator staggered, recovered, then jabbed Cam in the belly. Chase jumped into the fray and Tyler ended up in the pile.

Rhianna seemed to realize the distraction gave her a chance. She grabbed the judge's knife hand, yanked the weapon from her neck and thrust her high heel into her captor's instep.

Rhianna's moves gave Rafe an opportunity. Moving on pure instinct, he leaped over his brothers and father, landing within striking distance of the judge. Rhianna had freed herself, leaving the man a vulnerable target. He prayed the detonator wouldn't set off an explosion, but figured he had nothing to lose since the judge intended to kill them all anyway. In one satisfying blow, Rafe smashed his fist into the judge's chin.

Judge Stuart crumpled to the ground, unconscious. Rhianna flung herself into Rafe's arms. For a few horrible minutes, he'd thought he would never hold her again. He needed to breathe in her scent, let her warmth and softness heat his core. She was alive. She was okay. And he was one damn lucky man.

Sheriff Noel Demory stepped forward and handcuffed the judge. "We've got him nice and legal this time. He threatened to murder everyone here. He's going away for life. And it's just a matter of time until we round up the criminals who helped him kidnap Rhianna and steal the paintings."

Heart thundering in his chest, so loud he could barely hear, Rafe looked at Rhianna's bloodied neck, still in disbelief that everything had turned out so well. "Are you okay?"

"It's just a scratch." She was shaking like a one-year-old filly under her first saddle. "But I can't stop trembling."

"Who taught you how to fight like that?" Rafe asked, vowing to make sure they both taught Allison how to defend herself.

As his brothers and father separated, climbed to their feet and surrounded them, Rafe tucked Rhianna under his arm and against his side. "It's going to be all right. The judge will never bother us again."

Cam brushed at some dust on his father's shoulder. The senator rubbed his chin, but his gaze went straight to Rhianna and Rafe. "I asked for a diversion, not World War III."

Cam massaged his knuckles. "I always knew you

had a steel jaw. Had to make it look real.'' Then he glanced at his brothers. ''Why did you two jump in?''

''Didn't want to miss the fun,'' Chase replied sheepishly, ignoring his wife's frown at him as she handed Allison to Rhianna.

''Thought you might need help taking down the senator,'' Tyler teased.

Rhianna smiled at Rafe's brothers. ''We appreciate all the help.''

''That's what family is for,'' Tyler told her.

Rhianna's eyes shone with relief. She leaned against Rafe and he gazed proudly at their daughter sleeping in his wife's arms. He couldn't believe his luck. Or the happiness his two women had brought him. The years ahead looked bright. He gathered them both closer and looked forward to a future of sweet lullabies and good-night kisses.

HARLEQUIN®
INTRIGUE

opens the case files on:

TOP SECRET BABIES

Unwrap the mystery!

HARLEQUIN®

Makes any time special ™

Visit us at www.eHarlequin.com

HITSB

HARLEQUIN®

AMERICAN ◆ ROMANCE®

and **Muriel Jensen**

present

WHO'S THE
DADDY?

𝒜t a festive costume ball, three identical
sisters meet three masked bachelors.

ℰach couple has a taste of true love behind
the anonymity of their costumes—but
only one will become parents
in nine months!

Find out who it will be!

November 2000
FATHER FEVER #858

January 2001
FATHER FORMULA #855

March 2001
FATHER FOUND #866

HARLEQUIN®
𝒜akes any time special ™

Spines will tingle…mysteries await…
and dangerous passion lurks in the night
as *Reader's Choice* presents

DREAM
SCAPES!

Thrills and chills abound in these four romances
welcoming readers to the dark side of love.
Available January 2001 at your
favorite retail outlet:

THUNDER MOUNTAIN
by Rachel Lee

NIGHT MIST
by Helen R. Myers

DARK OBSESSION
by Amanda Stevens

HANGAR 13
by Lindsay McKenna

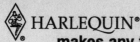

HARLEQUIN®
makes any time special—online...

eHARLEQUIN.com

shop eHarlequin

- ♥ Find all the new Harlequin releases at everyday great discounts.
- ♥ Try before you buy! Read an excerpt from the latest Harlequin novels.
- ♥ Write an online review and share your thoughts with others.

reading room

- ♥ Read our Internet exclusive daily and weekly online serials, or vote in our interactive novel.
- ♥ Talk to other readers about your favorite novels in our Reading Groups.
- ♥ Take our Choose-a-Book quiz to find the series that matches you!

authors' alcove

- ♥ Find out interesting tidbits and details about your favorite authors' lives, interests and writing habits.
- ♥ Ever dreamed of being an author? Enter our Writing Round Robin. The Winning Chapter will be published online! Or review our guidelines for submitting your novel.

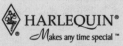